nicki's secrets

nicki's secrets

Mary Hooper

First published 2002 by Channel 4 Books
an imprint of Pan Macmillan Ltd
Pan Macmillan, 20 New Wharf Road, London N1 9RR
Basingstoke and Oxford
Associated companies throughout the world
www.panmacmillan.com

ISBN 0 7522 6202 5

A CIP catalogue record for this book is available from
the British Library.

Designed by seagulls

Printed and bound by Mackays of Chatham

This book accompanies the television series *As If*,
a Carnival
        films production made in association with
                Columbia TriStar Television for Channel 4.

Director: Brian Grant
Producer: Julian Murphy
Series devised by: Amanda Coe
Executive Producer: Brian Eastman

The End

There's a song about there being fifty ways to leave your lover. Only it's not that helpful when it comes to actually doing it, and no help at all when it comes to me getting shot of Toby Jarvis. As far as I know, there are only six – well, six main ways and a few subdivisions. Over the years, I've probably used most of them.

One

Tell them straight. I could say, 'I'm really sorry, Toby, but after sleeping with you I've kind of lost interest. I mean, you just don't *do* it for me.' This is good, because if you refer – however vaguely – to the Business, they get defensive and usually go without a fight.

nicki's secrets

Two

Say they're getting much too serious. This is pretty straight-forward, if a bit boring.

Three

Leave them, but don't tell them. Like, when you're supposed to meet them, be at the right place at the right time but... with someone else. Either be there with a girlfriend and just ignore him; or (better, but you've got to know what you're doing) be there with another guy. Either way, it usually ends in a fight, so don't wear good clothes.

Four

The l...o...n...g goodbye, where you make lame excuses all the time for not going out with him. By the time you've got to 'Have to stay in and clean out the gerbil's cage' he should have got the idea.

Five

Get a friend to tell him. This is OK, but I once got Sasha to tell a boyfriend that he was now an ex, and he ended up crying on her shoulder. The next thing I knew, they were dating. That really annoyed me, actually.

Six

I've never got this way to work properly for me. It's the 'I still really like you but only as a friend' way. It doesn't work because guys don't understand the concept of 'friend'. They think that once you've slept with them, there's no reason why you wouldn't want to again later – if you get bored, or no one else comes along. Which you might, but that's for you to decide.

I suppose another way is to write a note, but this doesn't make the list because the last time I tried it I got in a complete mess. Written down in black and white, 'I don't fancy you any more' looks so brutal. So I found myself writing pages about how it was probably my fault and there was absolutely nothing wrong with him and if only we had another time and place... etc. By the end of the letter I'd talked myself into going out with him again.

Toby

Toby was OK at first. For about twenty-four hours. Until we'd slept together. Then he got sort of clingy and started buying me chocolate animals and wanting to know what I was doing the whole time. When he bought me a teddy wearing a red heart on its jumper and started talking about what we'd do for our holidays next summer, I knew it was time for the big farewell scene. I mean, as if a twosome holiday was going to happen! Holidays are for meeting interesting foreign guys with sexy accents. And doing it on the beach with someone you're not going to bump into at the corner shop.

Giving someone the elbow is a pain, though. I'm not being big-headed here, but sometimes I think it must be easier to be like Sooz. Everyone knows she's never been out with a guy and no one fancies her anyway. If you don't get guys in the first place, at least you don't have to bother giving them the brush-off.

Funny, though – she pretends she's not bothered about having a boyfriend. She gets this superior little smirk on her face whenever I appear with someone new, as if she *could* have all that, but just doesn't choose to. Yeah, right. Not bothered, eh? So why the hours spent plaiting those dreads and sticking gold jewellery in your face then, Sooz?

While I've been wondering how to dump Toby, I've suddenly thought of another method.

Seven

The Poetic – for the more spiritual people amongst us.

'Toby, what we had was beautiful, but it just wasn't real life.'

'Toby, our love was much too precious to survive in this world.'

'Toby, I have to leave while I'm in love...'

I think that category's quite good, actually. I can go through all the books we're doing for A-level and snitch the best lines (OK, maybe not Conrad). Even better: I can choose a new author for each guy. This could go on for *years*.

That is, if I don't meet the love of my life along the way, of course.

Jamie

Jamie is making it pretty obvious that he fancies me. Like when he hears I've packed up with Toby (Method Seven) he tries to say he's sorry and all that, but can't stop this big fat smile coming over his face.

'It's OK,' I say. 'He wasn't that special. I mean, we weren't going to be like Sasha and Rob.'

Sasha and Rob. Mr and Mrs Loved-up. Or not right now, actually, because at a gig a few nights ago Sasha decked him one.

So after doing the condolences about Toby Jarvis, Jamie asks me to meet him in the Purple Turtle before going off to a party.

And asks everyone else to meet in the Spread Eagle.

Obvious or what?

I pretend to go along with it, but actually I've invited Rob down there too, thinking that I might get him and Sasha talking again. It doesn't work out like that, though. The three of us just get bladdered and don't get to the party at all.

Jiggy-jiggy

But about Sasha and Rob – something so weird. A couple of days after the Purple Turtle event, Jamie turns up again (he has this habit of appearing out of nowhere – think rabbit out of top hat). We're talking about Sasha and Rob and their problems, and Jamie is doing his I'm-a-sensitive-New-Age-guy bit, when suddenly he drops a bombshell.

'Sasha and Rob,' he says. 'No jiggy-jiggy.'

I laugh. 'Who told you that?'

'Rob did.'

'No! I don't believe it. You're winding me up, right?'

Because only a few days before, Sasha and I had been talking about orgasms – as you do on a Monday morning going into college – and she'd said to me that she needed a little extra help.

And of course, I thought she'd been talking about her and Rob in the sack.

'But we were only talking about... you know – sex – the other morning,' I say to Jamie.

He gets a funny little smile on his face and his eyebrows go up and down like a ventriloquist's dummy.

'Yeah?' he says. 'Sex? You and Sash? Girl on girl action?'

'You wish,' I say. '*They don't do it?* Why hasn't Sasha told me?'

Jamie shrugs. 'Search me,' he says. 'An' I wish you would.'

'Is it... like... Rob can't...?' I ask.

Jamie gets my drift and bristles a bit. 'That's my best mate you're talking about.' He flexes his muscles and does a little pouty thing with his lips. 'Shouldn't think there'd be any problem there. I mean, us guys... we're pretty hot stuff, you know.'

While I've been thinking about all this Jamie has been slowly moving his arm round the back of my shoulders. His face is entirely innocent — he actually thinks I haven't noticed. Suddenly I shake his arm off and stand up.

'I'm going to find Sasha,' I say.

'Oh. Are you coming back?' Jamie asks, but I'm too miffed to reply. My best friend — and she hadn't told me *that*! I have to find out what's going on.

Sasha

'Pig!' Sasha is shouting at the top of her voice.

I rush into the other room and she and Rob are facing each other. Sasha is — like — *glowing* with rage.

'You've got some nerve!' she says. 'Who else have you told?'

'What? What did I do?' Rob says. He looks at me. 'What's she going on about, Nicki?'

I open my mouth and close it again. I have a moment's panic. I have got it right here, haven't I? Jamie *did* tell me that they didn't do it?

'Leave Nicki out of this!' Sasha yells. 'This is between you and me.'

'I never...' Rob begins.

'Oh, you never! So someone else has put it about that I'm frigid, have they?'

'Sasha...' Rob begins.

I suddenly wonder if being an agony aunt is as easy as I've always thought.

Sasha looks round the room and says loudly, 'OK, for everyone's information it's Rob who won't do the deed, all right? He might go on like Mr Stud but you're all mouth and no trousers, aren't you, Rob?'

Everyone starts to laugh. Rob says, 'Sasha!' but she just marches straight out.

Rob rushes after her, and Jamie and I look at each other. I reckon he's thinking what I'm thinking: maybe we should have kept our big mouths shut.

Snog?

The row between Sasha and Rob puts me completely off my stroke for the rest of the evening. There are gorgeous guys at this party, but I just feel really cringy about Sasha.

Responsible, in a way.

When almost everyone has gone home, Jamie and I are sitting on a sofa in a corner. He's being quite sweet, actually, trying to make me feel better about what's happened. And looking at my boobs at the same time.

He thinks I don't know this.

He says that I've got to stop caring so much. That Sasha and Rob will get it sorted.

'Not by next Friday, they won't,' I say.

Jamie frowns. 'What's that, then?'

'The Mambo Room. The guest list. Rob's dad has got tickets and the three of us were supposed to be going.'

I realize this may make me sound a bit callous. So I'm just about to add that I'm desperate for Rob and Sasha to get back together, they're made for each other, when Jamie makes a move on me. Actually tries to snog me.

'Jamie!' I say, pushing him off.

'Sorry,' he said. 'I just misread the signals...'

'There weren't any! I don't fancy you, all right?'

It's best to be definite. But the thing is, it often makes them keener.

More Jamie

Picture this:

Jamie, nipping round behind the food counter at college to ask me if there's anything special I'd like to eat today.

Jamie, popping out from behind a postbox just as I'm posting a letter.

Jamie, deliberately crashing into me when I'm standing at the newsagent's stall choosing a magazine.

I blow up in the end. I mean, there's only so much of that cute smile and those puppy-dog eyes that you can take.

'I just want you to leave me alone, OK, Jamie?' I shout at him.

He's not a bit put out. 'Yeah. Yeah! Whatever,' he says.

He'll be back, though.

Zsa-Zsa

It seems to me that the smaller they are, the more expensive they get.

Pants, that is.

I'm in Zsa-Zsa, which is the most exclusive lingerie shop in town. We're talking mega-bucks for the tiniest suspender

belt, and what amounts to a mortgage for a negligee. I'm looking at the most gorgeous thing I've ever seen.

A thong.

Red lace and a scrap of organdie.

So beautiful...

I stroke it and one of the shop assistants glides up as if
she's on wheels.

'May I help you, Madam?'

'Just looking around,' I say, and she gives me a knowing
look. A look that says, hard-up student... don't waste my
time... get your grubby hands off the merchandise.

She's wrong, actually, because I *can* afford to buy stuff.
Thanks to Dad's allowance. If I wanted him to buy the shop for
me, he would.

But I move along, musing on the satin and lace bras: half
cup, full cup, platform, crossover, backless... every design
you can imagine. They're seductive – but not half as seductive as the red lace thong.

I have to have it.

But – hey, why should I pay for it? I could afford to... but I
don't like their attitude.

So as I pass the gold tray containing the thongs, I sweep
one up in my hand and squash it into a tiny ball. I pretend to

dab my nose, then push the thong into my pocket.

My heart is beating hard and fast... I'm *very* excited.

And if it excites me, just think of the effect that thong is going to have on the guys.

Sooz/tattoos

Sooz has a poster up asking for a bloke with a tattoo.

Sasha and I immediately thought she must be so desperate for a bloke that she has to advertise for one. But surprise, surprise – it's for her art and design project. Apparently.

I'm not keen on tattoos, myself. Especially if they're on a bloke, and they have another girl's name on them. Imagine that: lying in bed with someone and gazing at their chest or bicep and seeing a big love-heart with CHLOE or ANNA (or whatever) written there. Enough to put you off your lunchbox.

Simon

I'm in the pub, I'm wearing the red lace thong for the first time and I'm *so* up for it.

Simon – well, I've known him for years.

We used to sleep together but we've gone off the boil lately. He's more into discussing set text than sex.

But there's no one else around that I even half fancy, so I home in on him.

'Hi, Nicki,' he says.

I don't say hello. I just whisper, 'I'm wearing a red lace thong.'

His pupils enlarge.

Bingo.

Chris

Sasha is still not speaking to Rob. This is since the We Don't Do It revelation at the party. In fact, she's giving Chris the big come-on. Or he's giving it to her, I'm not sure which. Chris part-owns one of the clubs. He makes me feel kind of funny. Uneasy. I dunno... I don't like him. He's not the type I ever go for, but I'm kind of attracted to him. Not that I'd ever admit that to Sasha.

I heard him talking to her. He's so flash. Sasha pulled a condom out of her bag, and he said something about them needing more than one tonight.

'Guaranteed. Or your money back,' he says to her in his Mr Hot Chocolate voice.

Honestly. Guys like that, so sure of themselves – you don't know whether to smack 'em or shag 'em.

I don't know whether Sasha will get it together with Chris. I hope not. I think she's made for Rob and the sooner they get back together and start doing the business, the better.

Alex

When I'm with Alex this afternoon I almost try it on with him. Which is mad, 'cos he's as gay as a balloon. Well, he's such a good-looking guy – and I've always wondered if he's one hundred per cent poof.

So anyhow, he and I are sitting outside college in the sun and, just to find out if he's in the least bit up for it, I ask him if he's ever done it with a girl.

He looks at me, as shocked as if I'd asked him if he'd done it with a mallard. 'Nicki! Of course not. I'm gay!'

'I know that,' I say. 'What I was wondering was... how gay?'

He sits up straight and zips up his jacket. 'Very gay indeed, since you're asking,' he says. And then he giggles and I giggle. We end up rolling round the bench tickling each other.

He tells me about this guy he likes. Dan, his name is. He says he's the most gorgeous guy he's ever seen and he's got a Scottish accent and is simply divine all over.

'Have you seen him all over?' I ask.

He nods. 'Almost. I've joined his gym.' He puts his head in his hands. 'I made a right tit of myself. The running machine ran faster than me, I couldn't lift the weights and I went back-wards on the rowing machine.'

God, the things you have to do to get blokes when you're gay.

Party

Sasha and I are at a party and the red thong is having its second outing.

I'm not sure how we came to be here, actually. The party is at a friend of Chris's and Chris hasn't turned up yet. The guys are a bit older than us and I'm dancing and flirting with one in particular – Jason.

I've gone through a few seduction techniques but it's hard work, because the guy is telling me I'm not the type he usually goes for.

I reach up and whisper in his ear, 'I'm wearing a red lace thong.'

'Prefer black, myself,' says Jason.

'Who can tell the colour when you're under the covers?' I ask huskily.

I make him laugh, but it's not enough to keep him. His eyes are sweeping the crowd, looking for other pickings.

'OK,' I say quickly. 'You tell me what does it for you. Tell me, and I bet I can turn you on.'

He studies me, head on one side, and then he whispers, 'Girl on girl action.'

I look at him, startled.

I've always been one hundred per cent hetero. I never even had a crush on a female teacher at school, for God's sake. But if that's what it takes...

I whisper to Sasha. We giggle a bit. And then we kiss.

Jason is... well, shall we just say it does the trick?

 # Aggro

'I tell you, she just couldn't get enough of it.'

When you hear this sort of conversation, you just stop whatever it is you're doing and listen, right?

I'm in the café listening to Chris and Jamie talking, and it's pretty obvious that Chris is talking about Sasha.

'You know what it's like when a girl is just all over you.'

'Yeah,' Jamie says.

Yeah, right.

'She can't have been getting it from her last bloke...'

I shoot a look at Rob. Chris is mouthing off so loudly that he's heard everything.

Jamie is supposed to be Rob's mate. Why isn't he trying to shut him up? *'So are you... er... seeing her again?'* Jamie asks.

'She'll come running whenever I want her,' Chris says. *'I've got her in my pocket.'*

This is too much for me.

I go over there.

'That's my best friend you're talking about,' I say to him.

'Mind your own, OK?' he says.

Arsehole.

Still, my glass of red wine probably ruined his moleskin trousers.

Sasha

I try to tell her about Chris. I say that he's been dissing her to anyone within earshot. She says she doesn't care. That it's none of my business.

'You've screwed things up with my love life before, Nicki.'

'I'm just trying to help,' I say. 'Believe me, you're much better off with Rob. He respects you, doesn't he? Values you more as a person.' And then I think, why not be honest? 'And just for the record, Rob's much hornier.'

'Nicki!'

Bi-guy

I go to a club with Sooz and Alex and get off with a bi-guy. We only snog, but I really enjoy it. There's something fascinating about people who are bi. They're like aliens, really. They don't belong in either world.

I snog him and I know that Alex and Sooz are watching. Alex is grinning at me and I get the feeling that he's already tried the guy I'm with, and Sooz is affecting indifference but is probably trying to work out how to do it, and where the noses go.

Word on the street is that she's a virgin. This is so unsurprising.

While we're at the club, Alex's mobile goes and it's Dan, Dan the Wonderman. Alex goes completely to pieces at this because he's been waiting for a call all week, so when I've finished snogging the bi-guy, he and I spend a bit of time planning what he'll wear on his first date with Dan.

Sooz looks at us as if we're mad. Clothes R us but they're certainly not her. I couldn't even tell you what it is she wears; I think she just sort of covers herself up in the first thing that comes to hand.

High noon

Two days later, Sasha has seen sense. We're in the bar and she's heading for Chris.

She marches up to him and I'm just dimly aware of Alex at the bar too. All done up in Versace, his hair newly gelled and his face toned and balmed and shining like a choirboy's. It's the First Date.

Sasha is right in there, nose to nose with Chris. 'So I'm in your pocket, am I?' she says. 'Yeah, well, I've got news for you. It's over.'

Chris is cool. 'Nothing to be over,' he says.

With that, Sasha grabs him and spins him round.

Unfortunately she knocks Alex's Red Bull all over him as she does so.

'For what it's worth,' Sasha says, 'you were pathetic in bed!'

Alex is trying to brush himself dry. 'OK, guys. Take it easy,' he says.

Rob can't resist coming over. He and Chris trade insults, then he says, 'You've just been using her, haven't you?'

Chris says possibly the worst thing he could say: 'Yeah, well at least I know how to.' And at this Rob throws a punch and a fight breaks out.

Somehow, I don't quite know how, Alex's shirt gets ripped and someone digs an elbow into his nose, which bleeds all down him. I hurt my finger, Sasha shouts at Rob and storms off, Alex runs off into the night. All I can say is, he doesn't look nearly as good as when he arrived.

The end of a perfect night then. No snogs. No shags. And even Jamie seems to have deserted me.

Hook that guy (Tip 1)

The following day I pull out the stops and do the two-eyed wink at Jamie. This is more effective and not so obvious as the ordinary wink. What I do is glance at Jamie, then blink very slowly and smile. I wait for him to smile back, and then I look away.

This usually works. It's always worked before.

But it doesn't today.

Because, I find out later, Jamie has someone else. An older woman! Someone he met on the Internet.

He went salsa dancing with her and (so rumour has it) did it on the Embankment.

Alex had a good first date with Dan, too. But he's a copper, apparently, so Alex didn't dare tell him he's not eighteen yet.

Eighteen = age of consent.

He's real nervous about Dan finding out.

Je suis Serge

The music's loud, the man is French and gorgeous and I tell you, I'm really up for it. He's talking to Sooz for a bit and then she goes off and I think – *now.*

Hook that guy (Tip 2)

I deliberately turn my back on him. I wriggle — just a little — swaying to the music. Then I rub the back of my neck, up and down, up and down...

He comes over.

Quelle surprise.

He can't speak much English but who needs words? He has the most expressive eyes I've ever seen.

He burrows his nose into my neck and we play a little game of Guess the Perfume. So French! Imagine finding an English guy who can tell Gaultier from Goat.

We start dancing. Dirty dancing.

After a few moments I look at Serge enquiringly. I'm wondering what the French is for 'You're really doing it for me'. But I think he's got the message anyway. He gives me a Gallic shrug and a sexy smile and we go upstairs.

Nicki

The Casting Director
Cockney Folk
London

Dear Sir,

COCKNEY FOLK is my absolute favourite soap in the world
and I'm writing to ask for a chance to be an extra on it. Or
even have a small part with a word or two to say!

I have always wanted to be an actor or a model and regularly
take part in student reviews and so on. I am a Londoner and
feel I would be a natural on COCKNEY FOLK I enclose a
photograph and CV with my measurements.

I love the idea of being in a regular TV programme and feel
sure that I would get on well with the other cast members,
being both friendly and professional in my attitude.

I am willing to start at the bottom and take any sort of small
part. I would be very fast at learning my lines and – just so
you know I am not unintelligent – I'm taking four A-levels.

I can be contacted on the following email address:
nicki@hotstuff.com and look forward to hearing from you.

Yours sincerely,

Nicki

Limpet

I have a new top. It's got little coloured beads on it and is probably the most gorgeous top in the world. I am just admiring it hugely when the doorbell goes.

I know it's Louise (more commonly known as Limpet because of her habit of attaching herself when she's not wanted) and I know she's going to have a go at me. She was at the party where I made the French Connection. I rather abandoned her when I set eyes on Serge.

For a moment I think about hiding, but then decide I'd better get it over with.

She starts on me immediately. Apparently I don't think about anyone except myself, I put down my friends and – biggest sin – do not espouse values of sisterhood.

'You upset Sooz by barging in on the French guy, and then just left me wandering about on my own all night!' she says.

I'm offended. 'What d'you mean? I didn't know Sooz was after him. If she fancied a bit of French, why didn't she say?'

'I came up and tried to tell you, but you were practically doing it on the dance floor by then!'

'Yeah, it did get a bit heavy,' I say. I drift off, thinking about Serge and the interesting time we had under the coats on the spare room bed.

She's still glaring at me. In a moment of weakness I ask what I can do to make it up to her. She looks at my new top and I think, No! I don't want to make it up that much.

But yes, the top is what she wants. She puts it on and I have to say, it doesn't look nearly as good on her as it does on me. I think she must go to a chain store for her underwear. Still, as no one ever sees it, that's probably good enough.

We go to the café. Sooz and Jamie are there. He really does seem to have got over me.

Hook that guy (Tip 3)

I do the leg twine: slide onto a stool at the bar, cross my knees and then absent-mindedly stroke my calf and let my shoe half fall off.

Jamie doesn't notice!

I say sorry to Sooz for moving in on Serge. 'I didn't realize you liked him,' I say.

She shakes her piercings at me. 'Nicki, you're so shallow,' she says.

I don't reply. Shallow? I'm doing four A-levels, for God's sake.

Outside, I see Alex getting out of some guy's car. Some *gorgeous* guy's car. Must be Dan, I suppose. How come all the decent blokes are gay?

Zebra

Limpet starts on everyone straight away: her pet cause this week is cows in India and the leather trade. She wants us all to sign a petition.

I wouldn't mind, but as she's talking she's twiddling with the beads on my top. Yeah, of course I care about the cows, but I care about my top more.

'You're quiet,' Sooz says to me. 'What's up? Have Boots stopped running your favourite shade of eyeliner?'

I give her a withering look.

Jamie nudges me and nods out of the window. 'Why bother with the cows in India when there's slaughtered zebras lying right in front of us? Right, Nicki?'

I see what he means: the market stall over the road is selling zebra skin rugs. Fake, obviously. 'Right!' I say.

Alex joins us and we look in consternation at the stall. 'Yeah. Real zebras,' Alex says. 'That guy used to have a shop but it kept getting vandalized.'

Limpet looks at me. 'They're not really zebra skins, are they?'

I shrug. I so don't care. 'Why don't you go and find out?'

'Should I?' Louise says.

'Yes!' I say. To be quite honest, I am irritated to death with her.

She goes. I want to call after her to mind my top, but the others might think I'm shallow.

We all move closer to the window for a better look, and I notice that Louise has a bottle of ketchup in her hand.

'She won't do anything,' I say.

Just as I'm speaking, Louise sprays ketchup all over the rugs. The old boy behind the stall grabs her, and then this guy appears out of nowhere and puts an arm round Louise, like he's protecting her. I do a double-take: he is *gorgeous*.

A copper appears and Louise is nabbed.

'Oh my God!' I shout.

It's total crisis time. That ketchup will *never* come out of my top.

Sasha

We're having a bit of a girls' night in. Me, Sasha and a bottle of wine. I've been telling her about my *très magnifique* night.

'Let's just say I enjoyed my trip to France but I wouldn't want to move there,' I finish.

'You and men!' Sasha says. 'There'll be broken hearts all over Europe by the time you're finished.'

'You make me sound like some kind of slapper,' I say.

I wait for her to say, Of course you're not a slapper, but she doesn't. I ask about Rob – if they've made it up yet. She shakes her head.

'I blank him and then he blanks me... and all the time I can't stop thinking about him. I guess you can't help who you fall in love with, can you?'

Love and stuff

I'm just about to say no, you can't, when into my mind comes a whole line-up of guys' faces, one after the other. Like snap-shots.

Click! Toby Jarvis.

Click! Serge; Martin Taylor; Danny Williams; James Matthews; blond hair and glasses, didn't know his name; Terry Cross...

And I'm suddenly traumatized. *I have never been in love.*

Limpet

'I'm really sorry, Louise,' I say humbly.

I've been collecting money towards her fine. This will prove to her and to everyone else that I'm a good, concerned friend. I offer the collection, smile winningly and wait on her doorstep to be invited in.

She frowns at me; doesn't invite. 'What do you want?'

'I just want to say sorry, really — about making you go over to the stall and everything. And about the damage that was done.' I push the cash at her again. 'I've been collecting for the fine. Nearly everyone gave something.'

'No, thank you,' she says.

'It's just to help...'

'To help you feel better about yourself? I'd rather not, thank you.'

'No, I wanted to help out, as a friend.'

'A friend! A friend wouldn't land me in a police cell — and a friend wouldn't ignore me just because some cute guy made eyes at her. You're useless as a friend.'

'Oh!' I say, rather injured.

'And I'm not stupid, Nicki. I know you only go round with me when Sasha's busy!'

Before I can answer this she flings my top at me and

slams the door.

I slowly walk away, going over all she's said. Is it true — am I useless as a friend?

I look down at my top.

It's ruined, of course.

Rob

'No, it's over between me and Sasha. I've turned a corner.'

'I don't believe you, Rob. You two are meant to be together.'

'Believe what you like. It's finished.'

Well, I've tried.

Rob pushes my hot chocolate towards me. I grab it, and, as I turn away from the counter, bump straight into the good-looking guy I'd seen on the day Louise got arrested. He's got a flower stall just down the road.

Hook that guy (Tip 4)

I put my hand on his arm as if to steady myself. I leave it there a little longer than strictly necessary, looking into his eyes all the time.

'Like a bit of coffee with your cream, do you?' he jokes.

I've obviously got a blob of whipped cream somewhere, but this gives me an opportunity to lick my lips. Very slowly. Smiling up at him all the time.

'I ought to thank you for helping my friend,' I say. 'You know – the one who zapped the zebra skins.'

'Oh, that's OK. It's cool,' he says.

I glance over at Louise, who is sitting by the window with a face like a prune.

'She acts a bit mad, sometimes,' I say.

lose that guy

I'm about to make a move on him when he says, "Scuse me.' He actually goes *past me* to get to the Limpet. Open-mouthed, I watch him introduce himself as Gary, and see her go all twittery and apologetic.

I hear him say to her, 'It's OK. You stood up for what you believed in. Not many people do that these days.'

Well! I think. Who'd have thought he was a trippy-dippy tree-hugger!

Rob can see I'm put out. He grins at me and says, 'It's OK. Gary's kind go for girls like Louise. They like that caring, sharing strong belief kind of thing.'

'Thanks, Rob,' I say.

This is the pits.

I have been passed over for the Limpet.

I have never been in love.

I am shallow.

I do not have any strong beliefs.

It's obvious what everyone thinks: that I'm a self-interested slapper who doesn't care about anything except sex and shopping.

Well, I'll show them.

 # Showing them

Well, I *was* going to but it all happened so quickly.

I'm in bed.

I've just had sensational sex.

And... well, not to beat about the bush, I'm with Gary, actually.

Guess I'll have to show them some other time.

Sasha

At last I can be a real friend.

Sasha's got her house free for the weekend and Rob's coming round. So I sit down quietly with her and give her the benefit of my (considerable) knowledge of seduction skills.

Hook that guy (tips 5-9)

'If you've got an evening of seduction in mind, it's got to be well planned. Eat food that's an aphrodisiac – shellfish is good.'

'I'm allergic!' she says. 'You know that.'

'Burn scented candles...'

'They give Rob a headache.'

'Light a fire...'

'Hard. We've got storage heaters.'

'Have massage oil to hand...'

'Last time I tried that the sheets got slimy and my mum went mad.'

'Play some old-fashioned love songs...'

'Puh-lease...'

I look at her, exasperated.

'Thanks, Nicki, but I just feel we need a quiet evening in so that we can talk.'

'OK,' I say, 'but at least think about doing some of those. And *promise* me you'll be wearing a white thong.'

While she's thinking about this her mobile goes. The display screen says 'Chris'. Sasha shakes her head. 'Do you know how much I regret sleeping with that?'

'He's right up his own...'

'Yeah,' Sasha says.

I nibble my lip, thinking. Pouring that drink into his lap had been really exciting. I sometimes think about him grabbing hold of me and saying unbelievably filthy things in my ear.

And if he did that I'd kick him where it hurt. Of course I would.

Nicki

The Casting Director
24–7

Dear Sir,

24–7 is my absolute favourite soap in the world and I'm writing to ask if you would consider me for a walk-on part (or even a speaking part!) in it.

I am a regular viewer, know all the storylines and can assure you that I would fit into the cast like a dream! If you don't mind me saying, what 24–7 needs is a little more glamour. Why not give me a chance to show you what I mean?

I enclose a photograph and my CV with all my vital statistics. I am taking Drama as one of my (four) A-levels, am quick to learn and good at memorizing lines.

I would be willing to work for very little pay so as to learn the ropes and get on television.

I look forward to hearing from you,

Yours sincerely,

Nicki

The boyfriend

Limpet comes into the café, full of herself. She says 'Hi!' all round, very loudly and bouncily, just in case we might not have noticed her.

'Can't stop!' she says to me.

Did I ask?

'I'm just getting my boyfriend – getting *Gary* – a cappuccino,' she coos, as if buying coffee for a bloke is something rather special.

He had one at my house a bit earlier, I feel like saying. He certainly needed one after the session we had.

She goes out and Sasha looks at me. 'You should tell her he's two-timing her,' she says.

'What – and hurt her feelings?'

She can have him all to herself soon, anyway, because I'm getting just the tiniest bit bored with him. It's a shame, really. I *want* to fall in love but it just doesn't seem to happen.

Rabbit

All my hard work on Sasha's seduction techniques wasted.

Jamie. Turned up at Sasha's in a rabbit outfit.

How?

Yeah, you may well ask.

Apparently Sooz and Alex heard me and Sasha talking about the seduction evening, and they kidded Jamie that there was a fancy-dress party going on. He hired some ludicrous Bugs Bunny outfit and turned up just as Sasha was lighting the (unscented) candles.

They had the devil's own job getting rid of him, too. He just wouldn't take a hint.

All was not lost, though. When he'd gone they actually made it to the bedroom.

'And?' I say, eager for the finer details.

'It was brilliant,' Sasha says.

'Did the earth move?'

'You bet.'

I wish I had someone I was in love with.

Pizza

Inside my front door, on the table in the hall, are three large pizzas.

Triple cheese

Pepper and onion

Wild mushroom

None of them are touched.

Mum and Dad went out earlier, leaving me enough money to feed a family of twelve. So I ordered my usual Triple cheese – then, when it arrived fifteen minutes later, clocked the delivery boy.

Think Italian Stallion. Black gelled-back hair, green eyes and cheekbones so sharp you could cut paper on them. Name of Enzo.

When he went off to his next call, I slipped on the red thong and my dressing gown and ordered a Pepper and onion.

He brought it, we chatted for a bit – he's fresh over here from Milan – and then he went off on his bike again.

I ordered a Wild mushroom and we had another little chat. And now I've ordered another.

When he knocks I loosen my dressing gown, apply perfume and fluff up my hair before I go to the door. One look at the thong and he's all over me.

Hot Italian.

My very favourite sort of fast food.

Aggro

Alex has split up with Dan and is so cut up about it.

Sooz has got the hump about something.

Rob has fallen out big time with his dad.

Everyone's walking around like someone just died.

In fact, the more I see my friends, the less we seem to have in common. Sometimes I feel so much older than them. So much more in control.

Sebastian

This morning I realized that I'd managed, out of sheer indifference, to arrange three different things to do tonight.

- ★ Go out with Gary (he blew out Limpet specially);
- ★ Have a girls' night in with Sasha;
- ★ Go to a movie with Alex.

I'm just wondering which of these will be the least boring when this gorgeous guy walks into the café. I'd clocked him outside earlier. He drives a rather flash two-seater sports, and the best thing about it is that it's pale green instead of the oh-so-obvious red.

I rush up to the bar so I can stand there and look uncon-cerned and casual. I'm just wondering which of my little seduction tricks to try but I don't have to bother because almost immediately he asks me out to dinner.

Dinner! This is a new thing.

I've been to the cinema on a first date, to a meal in a café, a pub in the country – and to bed, of course – but never to dinner.

This guy – Sebastian – is very polite and speaks in what my mum calls a cut-glass accent. He says he has a dot.com company that's doing rather well. I can see that. He then asks me what I do – I say I'm a model.

'I was picked up by an agency just last month.'

'Fantastic!' he says.

I stare at him and practically melt. We are talking serious attraction here.

And serious money, by the looks of him.

'So let's celebrate your success,' he says. 'Dinner? Yes or no?'

'Well, I...' I pause for just a moment. 'OK.'

I would be utterly barking to turn down a guy like him.

He gives me his phone number scrawled on a book of matches and we arrange a time.

Hook that guy (Tip 10)

If you really want to impress the new guy you've just met, get a friend to ring you occasionally during the evening on your mobile.

I dress to kill, I'm ready on time and I'm in Sebastian's car when Jamie rings me and asks me what I'm playing at. I click my phone shut, and tell Sebastian that Jamie is my agent, and he's got me a booking in Prague.

He believes me. He pats my knee and says, 'Well done.'

We drive to a hotel. The car's top is down and the wind distresses my hair, but I don't mind being slightly ruffled. Neither do I mind other girls looking at me enviously as we purr by.

The hotel is huge and plush and shiny and gold. The chandeliers glitter like diamonds. There are enormous bunches of white flowers everywhere and tall church candles in glass holders.

We sit down and Sebastian orders the food and champagne. He's utterly charming and I am totally overawed. I just want to sit and look around me.

The food arrives and it's so beautiful, like a picture on my plate. I pick up the wrong knife and Sebastian puts me right. He says I'll get used to it – living in flash hotels and being in limousines. I tell him that I never want to get used to it. That I can't understand why all this is happening to me.

He thinks I'm talking about being a model. What I'm actually talking about, though, is being here. With him.

Sebastian says, 'It's happening because you are young and very beautiful.'

I smile at him. I've been told I'm beautiful before, of course, but what I always say is, everyone's beautiful sometimes. There are days when I do feel beautiful, and other days when I feel like a llama. Today, though, definitely isn't a llama day.

My phone rings again, I apologize and answer it. 'What's going on?' Jamie says. 'Aren't you supposed to be with Alex?'

'Yes – Prague!' I say. 'Staying in the Grand. Flying first class! I can't believe it.'

Jamie swears a bit at the other end of the phone and I say goodbye very sweetly.

When we've finished the most wonderful meal I've ever had, Sebastian asks the waiter to charge the bill to his room.

'Are you staying here?' I gasp.

He nods. 'It's not that exciting. After a while, these places begin to look the same.'

I look around. 'I'd never get bored with this!'

'I hope not. I hope you'll enjoy every single moment.' He lowers his voice. 'I'd like to ask you a question. Why are you so nervous?'

I gulp and shrug. 'It's just that the... er... last guy I went out with was a bit younger than you. I'm not used to all this.'

My phone rings again and Sebastian says, 'Leave it.'

He may be gorgeous but I'm not quite ready to do everything he says, so I don't leave it. I pick it up and listen to Jamie having a go at me, then Alex comes on and calls me a cow.

I switch off and smile at Sebastian. 'Friends. Can't get rid of them, can you?'

He takes the phone away from me and puts it in his pocket, then leans towards me and whispers in my ear, 'Stay with me. Stay with me tonight.'

'I'm not sure...' I begin.

For some reason I'm still nervous. I'm *never* nervous.

Sebastian kisses me. 'I'm jealous of every man who's ever touched you,' he whispers, and it's total meltdown.

The seduction

The hotel room is something else: sumptuous curtains and bedcovers, satin cushions and soft lights. The bathroom is white marble and there's a glass shelf with luscious-looking bath lotions and oils.

The evening seems much too wonderful to be true and I am strangely, unusually jittery. I shut myself in the loo and can't help comparing Sebastian to my usual blokes.

NO-HOPER	SEBASTIAN
Skateboard	Sports car
Broke	Stinking
Ten minutes max.	An hour at least. TBC
Pub	Posh hotel
Spag. bol.	Oysters
Lager	Bolly
Discount store	Ted Baker
Nike	Gucci
McJob	Real job
Cheesy talk	Sexy talk

Sebastian is everything I've ever wanted.

So why am I nervous?

What's my problem?

Answer: there isn't one.

He's just a bloke.

Push the same buttons – get the same results.

There's a knock on the bathroom door and Sebastian is standing there in a bathrobe, tantalizingly open around the middle.

He leads me towards the bed. I begin to say something but he puts a finger on my lips.

'No words...' he says huskily, and he begins kissing me.

The morning after

How can it all have gone so wrong?

Who can help me?

Sitting there in the hotel manager's office, I think desperately of someone to ring.

Mum and Dad? Out of the question. Jamie? Sasha? Rob? Alex?

Yeah, maybe Alex with his police connections...

OK, I know he's split up with Dan but it's maybe only a temporary split. Gay guys are notoriously temperamental.

nicki's secrets

I dial Alex's mobile but there's no reply. I can almost see what's happening: I bet he's in the café with the others, has seen my name on the display and is deliberately not answering.

I ask the manager if I can use his land-line, so Alex won't know it's me ringing.

Eventually he answers.

He *is* in the café. And I know they're talking about me because I hear the word 'slapper'. I plead with him and start crying.

Twenty minutes later he turns up in Jamie's mum's car. He's horrible to me.

'I know why you called me,' he says. 'It's because of my relationship with Dan, isn't it?'

I don't say anything. I'm too busy crying.

'Well, thanks a lot, Nicki! Were you so wrapped up in your own sordid little life that you didn't realize I'd actually split up with Dan?'

I blow my nose and shake my head. 'I'm sorry... really, really sorry. But I couldn't think of anything else to do. I mean, this is serious. He used my credit card and the manager's threatening to get the police involved.'

'What about your mum and dad? Can't they bail you out?'

'What? Tell them I slept with a con man? That'd really go down well.'

'You're the sort of friend I can do without, Nicki!' Alex says. 'Nice little corner you've shoved me into.'

Dan

'Now, let's get this straight,' Dan says. 'He stole your credit card and used it to foot the bill. Which was about six hundred pounds?'

I nod.

'When do you think he could have taken your card?'

I bite my lip, thinking. 'It could have been when my mobile rang at the table,' I say.

If I hadn't asked Jamie to ring me...

'I honestly had no idea!' I say to Dan. 'I didn't know! He told me he was staying here.'

He looks at me shrewdly. 'Know his name, do you?'

'Sebastian,' I say.

'Second name?'

I shake my head.

'Known him long?'

'Not really...' I admit.

'What does that mean?'

'Well... a day.'

I know exactly what he's thinking from the way he's looking at me.

The hotel manager asked me these questions, and with Dan repeating them it's doubly humiliating. I give Dan a little watery smile through my tears.

It doesn't cut any ice. He scowls at me and goes off to find the manager.

The awakening

While he's gone I turn the clock back to the moment I'd woken up, when everything had been wonderful... red roses, plump strawberries and the sun shining on the champagne bottle beside the bed.

I read the note on the pillow:

'Order breakfast and more champagne. Back soon, Seb.'

I'd stretched luxuriously, adoring every moment of it.

Knowing it was the way I was meant to live...

And then... then... I'd seen the empty clothes hanger on the chair and I knew he wouldn't be coming back.

lucky girl

I wait outside in the lobby while Dan and the hotel manager talk, and eventually Dan comes out again. He says that the manager has agreed not to press charges and is putting it down to credit card fraud.

'You're a very lucky girl,' he finishes.

I know it.

I try to thank him but he walks away.

Then I try and thank Alex and he blanks me, too.

Jamie's been waiting in the car outside, I tell him that it's not my fault; I just didn't think.

Jamie says that's just my trouble. That I see what I want and go for it without worrying about anyone else. 'But this time you've upset a load of people,' he says quite cheerfully.

'Thanks, Jamie,' I mutter.

Apparently Dan and Alex have split up big-time. Alex hoped they might get back together; but now that Dan has had to come and bail me out, it's confirmed to him that we're all just a load of kids.

How could I have known, though? And if they'd split up anyway, it's hardly my fault. But I don't say this. I don't say anything. Jamie drives me home, and I don't even flirt with him.

When I get home, Mum's out. I don't think her or Dad can have realized that I didn't come in last night. They were probably at each other's throats all evening, anyway.

Later on, I start thinking about Sebastian. I rummage through my rubbish bin to find the book of matches that he wrote his name and number on.

Actually, he is seriously gorgeous. He's a man of the world – OK, a con artist, but a man of the world. He knows about cars and wines and what knives and forks to use, he's unselfish in bed and he's utterly charming.

And OK, he may have pinched my credit card, but he really did like me.

I look at his number, pick up my mobile and put it down again.

Better not.

Nicki

To the Casting Director
Scallys

Dear Sirs,

SCALLYS is my absolute favourite soap in the world.

I'm writing to ask for a walk-on part (or even a speaking part!) on it. I've long been a fan and know all the characters, and so admire its gritty and realistic story lines. Maybe I could even suggest a few!

Although I live in London at present, I am very willing to relocate as I am determined to be an actress (or a model) and would be glad of any sort of experience. The fact that I come from London should not worry you as I am very good at Liverpool accents. Or maybe I could be a 'visitor from London'.

I am intelligent, friendly, professional and very quick at learning lines. I am taking four A-levels, Drama being one of them.

Please let me know if my letter is of interest. I enclose a photograph and my CV.

Yours sincerely,

Nicki

My friends

Three days ago I had five good mates. Okay, six if you count Limpet.

Now I've managed to lose them all.

Limpet – strongly suspects that I occasionally give Gary a seeing to.

Sooz – the cow is thick as thieves with Alex. She just said that I don't have to open my mouth to upset people. 'Just being alive and being here is enough.'

Alex – is still mad about rescuing me the other day. Clearly under the influence of above-named bitch from hell and thinks I'm selfish.

Rob – thinks I'm interfering too much between him and Sasha.

Sasha – so-called best friend, who bit my head off when I tried to explain more about Sebastian and the credit card. Said nastily, 'Oh, it's never your fault, is it?'

I am on my own in the café and am seriously fed up. The

market's closed so I can't even go over and flirt with Gary.

I ring Jamie.

I'm that desperate.

'I don't usually get like this,' I say to him. 'It's just that I could do with the company.'

Jamie comes up trumps. 'Yeah – well in times of emotional crisis, it's always good to seek physical comfort from a friend,' he says.

I hear his emphasis on the physical but I don't say anything. Just thanks, and that I knew I could rely on him. He says he's always here for me and I think, how *sweet*. He probably thinks there is more for him in this than a platonic hug, but I'll worry about that later. Who knows, he may even deserve a look at the red thong...

He turns up and we go for a walk. I'm thanking him sincerely for being there when I need him – possibly sounding a bit Oprah.

'My first thought was you,' I say.

'Well, after we've talked and all that,' Jamie says eagerly, 'd'you wanna see a film?'

This sounds like a date to me and I don't want to commit myself. 'Yeah. Whatever.'

'Tops!' says Jamie.

I'm just about to take his arm, when Rob appears.

Rob with a black eye.

'Don't say anything,' Jamie hisses. 'His old man did it.'

'Hi, Rob! You just caught us,' I say. 'We're off out.'

Rob looks pretty rough. His face falls and he turns to go.

I feel Jamie hesitate. Then he moves away from me. 'Wait up, Tiger,' he says to Rob. 'You look like you could do with a drink.'

Rob cheers up immediately. 'Yeah. Thanks, mate!'

Jamie says to me, 'Another time, right? Tomorrow? Whenever you like.'

'Sure,' I say. And I go off and leave them to it.

Friends? Yeah, right.

Sooz over

I'm at Sasha's and she and I are getting ready to go out.

And Sooz is coming with us!

This oh-so-unlikely event is taking place because Sooz came over to show Sasha the tattoo photos she'd taken of Rob, and they ended up swopping a photo for a gig ticket.

Sasha and I are astounded. I mean, the ticket was offered but we never thought she'd accept. Now we're lumbered...

I borrow a top from Sasha, use her mum's rollers and spend an hour or so doing the slap. Sooz does nothing whatsoever, just watches us curiously like she's observing creatures from another planet: Planet Girlie, as she remarked on entering Sasha's bedroom.

Sasha and I take in what Sooz is wearing and, with her eyes, Sasha signals to me: *Is she going in that?*

I signal back: *Surely not*?!

Delicately, Sasha says, 'Er... d'you want to borrow anything to wear, Sooz?'

Sooz looks down at herself. 'What's wrong with what I've got on?'

'Nothing!' we reply, rather too quickly.

I look at her and think, God, what a *mess*.

Why those dreads?

Why those piercings?

Why such a bitch?

I mean, what message is she putting out? Obviously cold. Frigid. Virginal. Never even been seen with a guy!

I stare at her, wondering what it would need to turn her into a halfway decent girl. Hair first. Cut off those dreads, get a bit of shine and a lick of gloss on what's left. Take out the piercings. Or OK, if she insists on having piercings, she can put them in her privates.

Expose legs.

Softer make-up.

Wonderbra.

Lessons in charm...

That should do it.

But even after that, her personality's not going to be changed, is it? She's not going to be sexy, warm, *nice.* Maybe she just doesn't like men...

We get to the club, it's crowded out, the music's brilliant and, strangely enough, we're all getting on quite well. Some guy starts to chat up Sooz but she doesn't realize it, and she confesses that she hasn't the faintest idea of how to get off with a bloke.

Who better to teach her?

Hook that guy (Tip 11)

'OK,' I say to her. 'Take that guy over there.'

'Who, *him*?'

'For demonstration purposes only,' I add hastily. The guy is a dork.

'You make eye contact with him. Look away. Then look back.'

'And finish by giving a little smile,' Sasha puts in.

The dork thinks his luck is in. He moves towards us and, shrieking with horror, we jump into the crowd and lose ourselves dancing.

Abandoned

I knew a girlie night out just wouldn't work. Sasha has spent the whole night texting Rob or talking about him, and now proposes to go home and leave me alone – with Sooz.

'I mean, it's not like she's going to cop off with anyone and leave you, is it?' Sasha says in a low voice.

We look at Sooz. She's trying out my sex tips for girls. You can almost hear her mutter under her breath: *Eye contact... turn away, then back... little smile...*

'That's not the point,' I say. 'We always used to say that best friends come before boyfriends. Now I so obviously don't!'

I turn away from Sasha and push my way across the dance floor.

'Nicki!' I hear her call, but I don't turn back.

I have a dance with a Japanese guy and idly start

planning a book entitled *Snog Around The World*. When we do kiss, though, to my disappointment it's not any different.

I abandon writing plans.

Jonno

I start wandering about looking for Sooz and to my amazement find her in the chill-out room *with a guy*. It's the same guy who tried to chat her up earlier, and the one she was trying out my Hook that Guy tips on.

Amazing.

I'm knackered so I plonk myself down between them and take off my shirt. 'So hot!' I say, fanning myself.

OK, my top's a bit low and skimpy and the bloke – name of Jonno – practically sits up and begs when he sees what I'm revealing.

I can understand that, though: half an hour of Sooz is probably enough for anyone. Wonder what they've been talking about?

I do not fancy him in the slightest but I naturally go into full flirt mode. I can't help it. It's partly who I am, and partly what guys expect. After a while, Sooz disappears to the loo and takes so long that I go looking for her.

'That guy is wondering where you've got to,' I say.

'Oh really?' Sooz says, heavily sarcastic. 'Well I was feeling a little green and hairy.'

Caterpillar? I think, and then I realize. 'Oh!' I say. 'You're jealous! My God. Was I doing it again?'

'Come off it, Nicki,' she says, and goes into one.

I blink at her. I hadn't even been *trying* with the guy. For instance, I hadn't even mentioned my Brazilian wax...

Sooz

We are walking home together. Sooz is striding out like she's power-walking and I'm trying to keep up with her. I feel a bit guilty – but honestly, how was I to know?

'I swear I didn't realize I was flirting!' I say. 'It's like an addiction.'

'Then maybe you should think about checking into rehab,' she snaps.

'You should have said. I wouldn't dump a mate for a no-hoper like him!'

As soon as I've called him a no-hoper I realize that maybe it wasn't the right thing to say. I gasp. 'Oh! You fancy him, don't you?!'

'Is that so incredible?' she says.

Bloody hell, *is* it?

'No! No, of course not,' I say quickly.

Sex and sandwiches

On the way home Sooz is starving so we call into a greasy spoon. While she's tucking into some form of pig sandwich, something occurs to me and I just *have* to ask her.

'Have you and Jamie ever... *you know*...?'

'Please!' she says.

'But you spend loads of time together.' Many's the time I've seen her in Jamie's shopping trolley racing down City Road.

'Yeah. As mates. Being with Jamie's a bit like having a pet.'

I know exactly what she means. 'But... well, I think I would, you know.'

'*Sleep* with him?'

'He's quite cute, really. Ever since that thing with Gabi he seems to have changed.'

Also... well, I know exactly what's made me put him up for consideration. The older woman thing, yes. But more him going off me.

I start to elaborate a bit more on the possibility of me and Jamie doing the do, when the door opens and in comes Jonno.

I make huge faces at Sooz. 'It's him! Here! It's like fate or something!'

'Get a grip,' she says, 'it's the only place open for miles around.' But I know she's pleased.

When he sits down with us I make my excuses and leave.

Besides, I find him deeply unfanciable and no, not even if you paid me, I wouldn't.

Domestic bliss

When I get home Mum and Dad are at it hammer and tongs. From the kitchen I can hear Mum yelling, 'I loathe the way you can never stop at one! If you have one pint you have to have eight!'

And Dad: 'I might not have to have eight if you didn't nag me all the time. It's the only way I get any peace. After six pints I don't hear you so well.'

I have heard this argument, with variations, many times over the years.

They don't notice me come in. I creep up to bed.

Nicki

The Casting Director
The Villagers

Dear Sir,

THE VILLAGERS is my absolute favourite soap in the world!

And I'm absolutely the sort of girl you want in it. It's a great TV show but I do feel you could do with a touch more glamour to make a pleasant contrast to all that mud. I am good at acting, dancing and different accents, and am just the right age to attract male viewers. I know in my heart I will end up being famous at something – either acting or modelling – and I would very much like to have THE VILLAGERS as my launch pad.

I attach a CV and photograph. I am hoping to have some glamour photographs done soon and I can send one to you if you wish.

I am taking four A-levels – one of them Drama – and am very willing to leave London and relocate.

I feel sure that if you give me a try, you won't regret it!

Yours sincerely,

Nicki

Virgin Queen

I am desperate to know whether or not Sooz actually lost it the other night. But the word from Alex is that she didn't, and no one must ask her about it.

What's wrong with the girl?

Why doesn't she just do it and get it over with?

Sasha and I discuss it and decide that she is definitely frigid.

Is this a medical condition?

Can you have treatment for it?

I shall never find out.

Babies

At last I've found out what's wrong with Jamie. He's been really odd, lately – almost offish with me. And last night, when we were trying to decide what to do, someone suggested salsa. We asked Jamie about it, because we know he's done it with Gabi (and salsa).

But he was preoccupied. Started talking about *pregnancy*, of all things.

Sasha said, 'You want to talk to Nicki about being pregnant. She was always pregnant!'

This is a slight exaggeration, but it's true that I used to have a thing about getting caught. I mean, the first couple of times that I slept with a guy I was certain he'd popped one of the proverbial buns in the oven – even if we didn't go all the way! I'm not like that now, of course. I'm on the double Dutch method: I use something and they use something. That way there can be no mistakes.

Last night we all agreed that we wouldn't want a kid for about ten years and then Jamie, looking stressed, went off. Today I interrupted a heart-to-heart between him and Sooz. Sasha wasn't around and I really fancied taking in a fluffy movie with a girlfriend.

Sooz? Well, she was the nearest thing.

So she gave Jamie the old heave-ho and off we went.

On the way she told me why Jamie had been so funny lately. Apparently he thought Gabi was pregnant – and that it was his baby!

It's not, naturally. They only did it once and they used something. But he still wants it to be. He's told Sooz that he's willing to take the baby whoever it belongs to.

Mad, of course.

Utterly mad.

When I get home, though, I think about Jamie some more.

All this Gabi business has definitely given him another dimension. He's not just a rock and roll animal. There's more to him than that.

Hmm. Interesting.

Goodbye again

I give Gary the old heave-ho.

I use Method Two. I say that our affair is getting much too serious. That, as I have a lot of things to do in my life, I don't want to get bogged down. As a bonus, I add a little touch of Method Seven: 'Kiss me one last time, then go and don't look back,' which I've borrowed from a poem and altered a bit.

Alex

Not having a love life of my own at the moment makes me extra-interested in everyone else's. So, when Alex starts filling me in on life in the gay community, I'm all ears.

'They're timing each other on the treadmills and soaping each other in the showers,' he says dolefully.

'Who are?'

'Dan and his new lover.'

I give him a consoling hug. At least he's not blaming me for the fact that he hasn't got Dan back. He tells me that instead of hanging around until Alex's eighteenth birthday, when sex and all that would be legal, Dan's found a guy his own age.

'They're two-by-two round the gym the whole time,' Alex says. 'They went in the steam room together and locked the door.'

'Blimey,' I say. I think about gorgeous Dan being soaped all over and have to fan myself. 'You gay blokes – you don't care what you do in public, do you?'

'The gym is safe,' Alex says.

'But anyway,' I say, 'you haven't exactly been Mother Teresa yourself.'

He looks at me. 'What – caring for poor people?'

'No! Laying off the sex!'

'I've been out with a policeman, then a fireman, and now I'm going out with a nurse,' he said, cheering up slightly. 'Jamie asked me if I was going through all the emergency services.'

Truth or Dare

At the club on Friday none of us manages to pull. In the case of Sooz this is not a surprise, but I have to admit it hasn't been the greatest snogfest for me, either. We have a few drinks instead. Not many, because none of us has any money.

Whether or not we've actually drunk a lot doesn't seem to matter much, though, because we're all acting completely rat-arsed when we go back to Sasha's house. She and I keep getting the giggles and Rob – well, with every giggle his face drops further.

I feel like doing something *mad*. And then Sasha suggests Truth or Dare.

Snog to your right...

'Yeah, let's do it!' I say, 'cos when gossip's a bit thin on the ground, Truth or Dare never disappoints.

Sasha gets a bottle and picks the dare, which is to snog the person on your right. We each look to our right to see who's there, and to think about whether a snog is going to be:

* ★ Desirable
* ★ Interesting
* ★ Revolting.

Jamie is on my right. He looks very pleased with himself.

And I'm on Sasha's right. Which could be interesting...

'...and the Truth,' Sasha continues, 'is to tell your most embarrassing experience at a party.'

She spins the bottle and it comes to rest pointing to me! Everyone cheers.

'Jamie, your dream's finally coming true,' Sasha says.

Jamie starts giggling and I can almost feel his temperature rising, he's so up for it.

But I decide to keep him on ice. 'I'm going to tell an embarrassing experience at a party,' I say, and everyone boos.

I tell some fairly innocent story. But then Sasha says, 'That wasn't the most embarrassing thing she's ever done at a party, though.'

I know what she's getting at and scream, 'Don't you dare!'

'Go on, you love it really,' she says.

I do, of course. But I cover my face. 'You swore you wouldn't tell,' I say, but actually I don't mind. It kind of enhances my reputation.

'She was with this guy...' Sasha begins.

'Jason,' I put in.

'But she just couldn't get it going with him. She tried and

tried... and in the end she had to ask him what really worked for him.'

'Yeah?' Jamie says with interest.

Sasha and I clutch each other, bent double with laughter. Everyone else looks interested except for Rob, who looks away.

'He wanted to see a little girlie action,' I say. 'So Sasha and I...'

'*You did it with Sash*?!' Jamie says. His tongue is practically hanging out.

'Of course we didn't do it!' Sasha says.

'We just kissed!'

'That was all it needed, though,' Sasha says. 'He couldn't get enough of her after that.'

Everyone laughs – except Rob. He does not look happy. In fact, he looks disgusted with both of us.

But that's not my problem. I think to myself, that's the downside of being in a proper love 'n' stuff relationship – you've got to consider someone else the whole time.

And snog to your left...

Sasha spins the bottle again. 'The dare is to snog the person on your left. And the truth is, who in this room do you most want to sleep with?'

The bottle ends up pointing at Sooz and we all hoot.

'You cheated!' Sooz says. 'You did that on purpose.'

'No, I didn't!' says Sasha. She looks triumphant. 'Come on – tell us! Who d'you most want to bed?'

'Is it animal, vegetable or mineral?' Alex asks.

'It's not a difficult question, Sooz.'

'Well, it is if she's trying to name someone who might fancy her back,' I say.

Sooz looks fairly desperate. Then she and Jamie suddenly fall on each other and do this big tongue job.

'You look like you enjoyed that,' Sasha says, when they come up for air.

Sooz pulls a disgusted face, but I'm not sure if she's putting it on.

'Is there something going on between you two?' I ask. I can't help feeling the slightest bit niggled. He always used to like me best...

'No, don't worry, Nicki,' she says sarcastically. 'He's all yours.'

Darkest secret

The bottle is spun again. Sasha calls out, 'The truth is, who did you lose your virginity to and where?'

'No. Your darkest secret!' Sooz says quickly. And I know exactly why she's said that. Because she's still a virgin! Imagine that. Imagine being eighteen and still untouched. That's obviously *her* darkest secret.

Chris

I'm hoping the bottle will stop at Sooz so we can really do some digging on her. But it doesn't, it stops at Alex.

'Come on, your darkest secret!' says Jamie gleefully.

'Well, it's to do with Chris,' Alex says, after a moment's hesitation.

'Yeah, don't tell us – he's gay!' I say.

Sooz blinks in Sasha's direction and says pointedly, 'Well, we all know that's not true, don't we, Sasha?'

'Well,' says Alex, grinning. 'You might just have sussed it.'

'You're joking!' Jamie says.

'He'd kill me if he knew I was telling you...' Alex lowers his voice. 'It was tonight, in the club. I went into the toilet and he was there, with his arms round some guy.'

There are gasps of disbelief all round.

'No!' I say. We all stare at Alex.

'You're winding us up,' Jamie says.

'No. I know the bloke he was with. He goes to the gym, if you know what I mean.'

'You sure that he's...?'

'Look, he's a poof! A card-carrying poof!'

Rob has cheered up considerably. 'And you definitely saw him with Chris?'

Alex says yes and we all sink back and try and take this in. Chris – gay? Or bi, maybe. I already know how I feel about bi-guys. And I'm going to take this little secret home and try to work out how I feel about Chris now that he might be bi. He's still a bastard, of course. But I can't help thinking he's a rather more interesting bastard than he first appears.

The game goes on...

... and we all start bickering a bit. It's almost morning, and we're tired and a bit hysterical. Sasha and I are, anyway.

When the bottle points to Sooz, she neatly gets out of telling how she lost her virginity. Somehow (don't ask) her dare turns out to be her and Rob running round the streets in their underwear.

They get undressed and we all stand at the window, screaming and yelling them on. Then they disappear from view – and are actually gone rather a long time. I know Sasha's getting uneasy, wondering what they're up to, 'It's OK, the poor cow's frigid,' I remind her.

When they eventually arrive back and get dressed, Rob clearly wants to go home. Sasha and I yell for one more spin of the bottle, though. It points to Jamie and he has to tell his most intimate moment with a partner.

Gabi

'Course, he wants to talk about Gabi but we don't give him a chance.

The thought of Jamie having any sort of intimate moment is completely hilarious – don't ask me why.

'I still love her,' Jamie protests. 'I would have been a father to the baby. I would have looked after it. Even if it wasn't mine!'

Sasha and I roll our eyes at each other. We want funny confessions, not sob-sniff ones.

Carl Thompson

I grab the bottle and spin it. 'OK. The worst thing you've ever done with a partner – or show us your privates!'

The bottle ends up pointing to Sasha.

'Privates! Privates!' I yell.

Jamie perks up a bit.

But Sasha wouldn't dare – not with Rob around. She thinks for a moment and then she says. 'I've got it. The worst thing I've ever done with a partner – it's got to be Carl Thompson. He was so useless in bed...'

'Really!?' I say.

'Yeah! He was pushing this and pulling that and when the moment came – there was nothing there!'

I let out a piercing scream.

'I was really bad, you know,' Sasha continues. 'I was laughing and laughing at him and he was apologizing. I said, "Do you know what – you're a sexual retard!"'

Sasha and I dissolve, but the others don't laugh or say a word. Actually, they're looking embarrassed.

As for Rob – well, he gets up and slams out of the house.

And then Sasha runs after him and the rest of us go home.

Rob ... and Sooz?

Sasha calls me late the next day to say that she and Rob had a huge argument. Apparently he called me a tart and said that she was getting just like me – telling half the world who she'd been doing it with.

This using 'tart' as a derogative makes me so bloody mad. If a guy sleeps around he's a stud and a stallion. It's an excellent, *phhwor* kind of thing. But if a girl sleeps around it's all sniggery and tacky, she's a trollop and a slapper.

I tell Sasha that Rob ought to lighten up a bit. That we'd just been having a laugh.

Later I think about Rob and Sooz. Throughout the evening I'd noticed her looking at him...and they were an awful long time, running round that block.

Is there something going on between them?

I daren't say anything to Sasha. She'll tear Sooz limb from limb and ask questions afterwards.

Truth or Dare - Discoveries

Altogether, a very interesting night gossip-wise:

★ Rob is a moody bastard who doesn't like Sasha enjoying herself.

★ (a) Jamie is hung up on Gabi, but (b) still fancies me.

★ Chris is bi-sexual.

★ (a) Sooz is most definitely a virgin, and (b) possibly – there is something going on between her and Rob.

S and M?

'Just an apron?' I say to Jamie in horror.

'And rubber gloves,' he mutters.

'No!'

Alex and I both stare at Jamie, who's come into the café looking like he's been plucked out of a morgue and dropped into Ladbroke Grove as a social experiment.

I pass a hand across his face but he doesn't react. It's like he's in shock.

A while back he found out about a night job at a posh hotel – they were having some special dinner or other and wanted silver service waiters. It was quite good money so Jamie asked if any of us wanted to go with him.

I didn't, of course. I do not do 'waitressing'.

But he, Sooz, Rob and Limpet went and apparently the maître d' was a good-looking woman who also happened to be a raving perve. She had the hots for Jamie and after the ball was over, so to speak, jumped Jamie then tied him up and humiliated him.

In the nicest possible way.

'Jamie, are you all right?' I ask, but he's not with us. 'I mean... did you *enjoy* it?'

I have never gone in for S & M myself.

Nor M & S, come to that. I think they're both more middle-aged things.

'Ahh-huh...' Jamie murmurs.

I go off to get a coffee, first whispering to Alex that he's got to find out every last detail.

Rob and Sasha

Apparently, all is not right between them.

Again.

Sasha's told me that Rob didn't get in from the hotel job until the small hours, and then turned down the offer of scrumpy in the shower. She says he's been acting odd – odd in the way of wanting to wash his clothes as soon as he's taken them off, and odd in the way of illicit phone calls.

I am still wondering whether it's anything to do with Sooz.

She plays the ice maiden, but ever since the running-round-the-streets-in-your-keks night I've been watching her watching Rob.

 # Finding out

So, a bit later, when Jamie is looking only half-dead instead of all dead, I try to pump him for info.

'Rob and Sooz,' I say. 'D'you reckon there's anything going on?'

He looks at me, alarmed. '*What*?' he says. 'What d'you mean?'

I lower my voice. 'Them two... just something I've been thinking about. Women's intuition an' all that.'

'You're mad!' he says, with way too much certainty. 'Them two! Not in a month of Sundays. Completely out of the question! Ridiculous!'

'Hmm,' I say. If there really *had* been nothing to it, he'd just have just shrugged and said, 'Nah!'

Methinks he went on just a little too much.

Limpet comes in and – knowing she was actually there last night – I make a bee-line for her. 'Sooz and Rob...' I say in a low voice.

'What? What about them?'

'D'you think anything might be going on between them, Louise?'

She frowns. 'Of course not. Sooz wouldn't trunk in on another girl's boyfriend. She has got morals, you know, Nicki.'

'Don't be so naive!' I say.

'Just because you...'

I sense a lecture about sisterhood coming on, so I say quickly, 'Didn't you notice anything odd between them last night?'

She thinks, and then she says, 'Now you mention it, it was a bit funny.'

'What was?'

'They disappeared – Rob and Sooz. They were mucking about and the maître d' told them off. So they just quit with a bottle of champagne.'

'*Really*?' I say. 'Where did they go?'

'Home, I guess,' Limpet says.

'But he didn't arrive back for hours...'

She looks at me, shakes her head. 'As I say, Nicki, you

shouldn't judge everyone by your own standards. Rob really loves Sasha. He'd never do anything to jeopardize that relationship.'

'Oh. Right,' I say.

Would a bloke turn down a quickie?

Does a bear pooh in the woods?

Limpet goes out again (she's at her favourite occupation, getting coffee for Gary). I go and chat to Alex so we can pour over the evidence together. Alex doesn't know anything about Rob and Sooz, but he loves a bit of gossip.

 # Surprise!

Suddenly Sasha breaks off from the big heart-to-heart she's been having with Rob and rushes over to us.

'Nicki! Hey guys! Rob's just asked me to move in with him!'

'Fantastic!' Alex and I say together, and I give her a big hug.

She looks so happy that it would be horrible of me to carry on thinking what I've just been thinking.

But I do...

And as Sasha's telling us, out of the corner of my eye I see Sooz get up and go off to the loo. She's crying.

Rob comes over and I hug him, too, and we talk about

where they're getting the money from (Sasha's mum) and where the flat might be. Sooz comes out of the loo, pretends to look surprised and pleased at the flat news. Then, a moment or two later, she goes off with Jamie.

I watch them walking down the road together. He's got his arm through hers, as if he's comforting her. He's holding her close.

What's been going on?

Nicki

The Advertiser,
Box 390

Dear Sir,

I am writing in response to your advert for dancers/models.

I haven't had much experience but I'm a terrific dancer (I've had some training in classical ballet) and I learn fast. I've always wanted to be a dancer or a model and I am willing to work in any country; I have no ties.

I'm at college doing four A-levels at the moment (so you can see, I'm intelligent, too!) and I have various options to work in several of the TV Soaps. I am expecting to hear something very soon about these.

I enclose a photograph and my CV, and though it doesn't look as if I've got much experience, I am very willing to learn. I haven't any professional photographs at the moment, but I'd be quite happy to visit you (in London, presumably?) for an interview.

I look forward to hearing from you.

Yours sincerely,

Nicki

Alex

It's Alex's birthday.

We've been trying to cheer him up for some time. I even took him shopping – what could be better than that? But he's still in the doldrums and it's all because of Dan.

He tried to tell us that he was enjoying the process of forgetting, and that it was all part of the grieving process. He also said that he didn't want any fuss on his birthday.

But no one believes any of those things, so we're having a party tonight.

Jamie is ringing Dan and trying to persuade him to come, Sooz is keeping Alex out of the way, and me and Sasha (when she can stop snogging Rob) are getting stuff ready at H2O, where the party is going to be.

I haven't managed to find out anything more about Sooz and Rob. Is there anything to find?

I don't know.

The evening starts brilliantly. Sooz pretends to Alex that they're just going for a couple of drinks and when they arrive at the club we're all there, bobbing our balloons at him and cheering like mad.

Alex is really chuffed. In fact, he looks happier than anyone's seen him for ages. Trouble is, he's turned up with some guy called Jeff.

'Who's *that*?' I ask Sooz.

'Dunno. I asked Alex round for a few drinks and he turned up with *him*.' She pulls a face. 'From the way they've been talking, I think Jeff's his new boyfriend.'

I suddenly notice Dan advancing across the dance floor. He's actually come! And he's bought Alex a present.

Alex beams all over his face when he sees him. Jeff's nowhere around so he and Dan go into a huddle and everything seems to be hunky-dory. I don't know what will become of Jeff but hey, so many guys, so little time...

I spot Chris and go and chat to him. Since Alex told us the thing at the party – the dark secret – I've been quite intrigued by Chris. Macho and bi-sexual together. Quite a combination...

Chris

He looks me up and down.

'That's a wicked outfit,' he says. And you know the expression, 'He undressed me with his eyes'? Well, Chris was positively *ravaging* me with his.

I give him a sidelong glance. 'You into women's fashion, then?' I say, because I suddenly wonder whether he's the type who likes getting togged up in suspender belts and black lace.

'What?' he says.

Hook that guy (Tip 12)

Move into his space. Stand so close that you're almost touching... let him feel your body heat. If you stand close enough for him to kiss you, he probably will...

When I've moved in real close, Chris gives me a slow smile. 'Hey,' he says softly. 'I thought you didn't fancy me.'

'That was before I found out,' I say.

'What? Found out what?'

I moisten my lips with my tongue, just a little. 'Well, I've always been fascinated by bisexual men.'

'What?' Chris looks amazed and not a little shocked. I think back to Truth or Dare. Yeah, that's definitely what Alex had said.

'Bisexual men... er... fascinate me,' I say, but with less certainty.

'Me?'

I nod.

'Me a poof?'

Now I am not at all certain.

'Well... that's what Alex told us...'

Chris still looks shocked so I add quickly, 'Not that anyone's bothered... I mean, we've always known that Alex is gay. Stuff like that doesn't matter, does it? Gay, straight, bi – if you ask me it gives some guys an edge.'

'Where is he?' Chris says. 'Where's Alex?'

I shrug. 'Don't know...'

Chris goes off in search of him, looking angry enough to ignite. I'd like to help but I somehow don't think that saying anything at this stage is going to do any good.

And, well, it's not my fault, is it? Alex must have got his wires crossed.

Consequences

I mingle in with the dancing crowd but get near enough to Alex to listen in. It's already clear that Alex and Dan aren't exactly getting on well. Dan thinks Jeff is Alex's new lover... after Jamie had assured Dan that Alex had been leading the life of a nun.

Or a monk, maybe that should be.

Chris goes right up to Alex and confronts him. 'What you

been saying?' he asks aggressively. 'You spreading it around that I'm a shirt-lifter?'

I wince. Chris is not exactly PC.

Alex's jaw drops. 'No, I...'

'That's what Nicki says.'

I shrink even further, trying to make myself as inconspicuous as possible.

'She said you've been telling people I'm a poof.'

'No! No, I...' Alex spreads his hands. 'Look, I saw you with this guy in the toilets last week. You were hugging. I just sort of thought...'

'Well, I'm not. But *you* are, aren't you? Why didn't you say? You thought I'd have a problem with it?'

'No,' Alex gulps.

'You should be more honest with people if you want them to trust you,' Chris says. 'I would still have lent you the money.'

I already know about the money. Alex borrowed it from Chris so he could hold his own with Dan – pretend he had a well-paid job.

Alex shoots a look at Dan. It says that his whole life is unravelling in front of him.

'Not now, though. I want my money back,' Chris goes on. 'Gimme what you got now. I want the rest by the end of next week.'

Dan comes back into it.

'This guy bothering you, Al?' is all he says, but I'm trans-fixed. God, that Scottish accent just does it for me. So sexy!

'Mind your own,' Chris says to him rudely.

'I'd watch your mouth, pal,' Dan says, and I'm just about to take my seat at the ringside when Alex makes peace.

'It's OK,' he says, handing Chris some money. 'It's his. I owe him.'

Chris says nothing, just pockets the money and goes. Dan and Alex talk a little more, then Dan goes off.

Snogs: nil.

Shags: nil.

Not a brilliant evening.

Phone call...

'Is that Nicki?' a man's voice asks.

'Mmm,' I say cautiously. (Well, you never know when your past is going to catch up with you, do you?)

'You wrote to us. To my company.'

My heart jolts. I've written loads of letters over the past two years but I've never had a reply.

Not one.

'Who are you?'

Royal Shakespeare Company? Would they be ringing at nine o'clock at night? ITV? No, better not hope for that.

He coughs. 'I'm Mr James. You wrote to me about being a model.'

'Yes!' I say eagerly. '*The Advertiser* – last week. What sort of modelling is it? I'm a perfect size ten.'

'Modelling and dancing,' he puts in.

'I'm a brilliant dancer. I've done ballet in the past.' He doesn't say anything to this so I add apologetically, 'My mum made me go when I was three. I can do *all* sorts of dancing, though – modern, classical. I pick up routines very quickly.'

'Perhaps you'd like to come along and see me, then.'

'For an interview? Brilliant!'

He gives me a time (next week), and a place (north-west London). Unreal!

Although I'm fantastically excited and want to practise doing dance moves, I sit down and think about what I'm going to wear, and how I'm going to look.

This is my one big chance and I don't want to blow it...

Result

I can't believe it!

Straight A's.

Four of them.

Shallow? Me? I don't think so. I mean, I know it's only Mocks, but still...

Sooz looks at me and obviously wants to drive a stake through my heart right there and then on the steps of the college. But the others are around, so she can't.

She hasn't done very well – I can see that – but I'm much too thoughtful to ask her exactly *how* she's done. I'll find out later.

I go home and want to celebrate, but Mum and Dad are having a row.

Now there's a surprise.

Sooz

The day after the results, Sooz rings my mobile. I am amazed at this (but realize later that she has rung me in desperation – the others are out).

Five minutes later she's standing on my doorstep wearing a T-shirt.

That's it.

Just a T-shirt. Apparently she's locked herself out and her mum won't be in until much later, so she wants to borrow some clothes.

From me!

I have visions of dressing her in glitter, in a fake fur microskirt or lace hot-pants, in fact in something extremely tacky. But I don't do tacky. Everything in my wardrobe has style.

I do girlie, though.

First of all I try her with a very short, tight skirt, but she has what amounts to Clapham Common growing on her legs and she refuses to wax.

So I put her in plaid trousers.

Then I try to get her T-shirt off, but she won't let me glimpse flesh. I make a joke about us being girls together, but she still won't. Someone's going to have a pretty hard job getting her to relinquish that virginity.

I give her a top to put over the T-shirt. A Gucci top.

And finally add some *pink* shoes.

Pink! Pink and Sooz. Not an obvious combination...

She looks pretty different. Now I'm just going to stand back and see what happens.

Light...

'Cor!' Jamie says, looking Sooz up and down.

'You like?' I ask.

Sooz kind of shrinks into the nearest chair. 'They're not mine!' she says to Jamie. 'I got locked out. Nicki lent them to me.'

'Don't apologize,' he says. And he looks at her as if he could actually fancy her!

...the blue...

'Wow!' says Sasha, looking at Sooz across the café.

'Barbie gone wrong!' I say.

'I love it!'

'Least it looks a bit more female now.'

Sasha snorts. 'Don't care what you say. Still looks like a man in drag.'

We giggle.

...touchpaper

Sooz and Jamie are chatting.

They are sitting quite close to Sasha and me.

But not that close. I mean, it wouldn't be difficult for Sooz to keep her voice down, but she obviously wants Sasha to hear her. And I wonder if this is because she's heard me and Sasha laughing about her and wants to get her own back.

Jamie is saying to her, quite low, 'I saw you both at the hotel.'

'*He* kissed *me*, right?' Sooz says. 'Not the other way round.'

I know straight away that it's Rob they're talking about. And Sasha knows too, because she signals the shock to me with her eyes.

'It doesn't mean he's in love with you,' Jamie says.

'Who said anything about love, Jamie? I didn't!'

I can't hear the next bit, then Jamie says something about not letting one kiss affect her. Sooz, nearly in tears, says, 'Don't laugh at me! D'you hear?'

Jamie says, 'Sssh, Sooz, you're in a right state. Sort it out or you're gonna get hurt.'

Sooz just gets up and goes into the loo and I look at Sasha.

'Don't say a word,' she says. 'Not one word.'

I *knew* there was something up, I just *knew* it, Sasha goes over to Rob and starts mouthing off to him. He protests, but she won't back down. It ends with her saying that he and her are done for good this time.

She walks out.

Smoke

Rob looks gutted. Then Sooz comes out of the loo and talks to him. The vibes don't look good for her, though. I mean, I can see from his body language that he doesn't fancy her. Why don't girls learn about stuff like that? It saves an awful lot of trouble.

Rob goes outside and Jamie follows him. Through the window I see them having a heart-to-heart. As much as guys do, any rate.

Then Rob comes back in and he starts talking to Sooz. A deep meaningful talk. They seem to reach some sort of agreement – but just as Rob is giving her a quick hug, *Sasha comes back in*!

I think that Sasha is going to deck Sooz, but she doesn't. She just turns around and goes straight out again.

Now Rob looks desperate.

Sooz looks desperate, too.

It's at times like this that I'm glad I've never been in love.

Night of the long knives

Sooz is lying on the floor, apparently dead. Limpet is next to her, also dead.

Well, that's how it looks at first.

We're at the town swimming pool. Rob got the keys... then he lost them and we found ourselves stuck.

We're doing this spoof film for college, and we borrowed a camcorder and equipment. But Limpet found out that we were all going off without her, so she followed us to the pool. She then fell through the window – cutting herself and smearing blood everywhere.

When we all thought we heard some ghostly noises, Sooz ran off in fright, slipped, and fell down next to Limpet. So when we came round the corner and saw them both, it looked like...

But it's not.

They're both OK.

Limpet sits up and gives us a whole load of grief, and we call an ambulance and off she goes to be looked at.

Sooz picks herself up and we go home.

On the way I whisper to Sasha, 'Bet you thought your troubles were over when you saw Sooz lying there...'

'What d'you mean?' she says. 'I'm not scared of Sooz! Rob wouldn't look twice at that little bitch.'

'No! No, I know he wouldn't,' I say hastily. Sooz had been round to tell Sasha that there was no way that Rob could possibly be interested in her. And that nothing at all had happened between them, except in her imagination.

Sasha believes her.

I don't.

The interview

'Get your kit off,' says the man – Mr James – when I'm standing in his office. It's a poky room up four flights of stairs, which looks like it's never had the benefit of a cleaning lady.

I glance out of the window. I can see roofs and chimneys and some blacked-out windows.

''s OK, no one can see in,' he says impatiently.

He's older than I thought, and he's got one of those noses that are red and lumpy. I think it means he's over-indulged in something or other.

I pull my top over my head. Bet he hasn't even noticed it's Ghost.

I stand in front of his desk in my bra and come out in goose-pimples. There's stripping for a man and stripping for a man.

This is the second sort.

'Nice,' he says. 'And the rest, please.'

I hesitate. He says, 'Look, I'm a very busy man. Bra off and down to your pants.'

I still hesitate. I'm wearing my lucky red thong – but then I hadn't realized I'd be stripping off. If I had, I'd have worn something a bit less revealing than two centimetres of red lace.

'Bloody hell, you're not going to be like this for the punters, are you?' he says.

'No, I – *what punters*?'

'You'll be dancing in front of sixty men, darling.'

'Yes, but...'

'Pole dancing. You've heard of it, haven't you?' He guffaws. 'What you do is, you wrap your fanny round a pole – only you do it artistically. To music.'

I pick up my Ghost top.

'Thank you for seeing me,' I say politely and icily. 'I won't be taking the interview any further.'

I hear another guffaw as I trip down the stairs.

Goodbye again

'Tonight?' Danny says.

I shake my head. 'I don't think so.'

'Tomorrow, then?'

I put my head on one side, looking regretful, yet fond. (I have already selected Method Two.) 'I'm really sorry, Danny. I just think... well, you're getting much too serious for me. I'm not into all that commitment stuff...'

At the door, he tries to persuade me again to see him, but I gently kiss him on the cheek, whisper goodbye and move off.

All in all, quite a successful leaving.

Chris

Danny lives in a small block of flats. Outside in the street, I bump into Chris – who's just come out of the flat below Danny's. OK, he's obviously not bisexual, and I don't actually like him – but there's still something jaggedly fascinating about him.

We grin at each other.

'You're up early.'

'You're out late.'

'Just visiting a friend,' I say.

We have a bit of banter, throwing digs at each other, and I end up saying (rather suggestively), 'Let's not pretend we like each other, Chris.'

In that case he won't offer me a ride home, he says; I say I prefer to walk anyway. It keeps me fit.

'I'll say!' Chris says, and I know – just know – that as I walk away he's ogling my bum.

I think about him all the way home.

I can't resist a challenge.

But first I have to check him out with Sasha.

Check

'You are over him, aren't you?'

Sasha looks at me in amazement. 'I can't believe you even had to ask.'

'It's just that – I know he upset you and you've never really talked about it.'

Sasha shrugs. 'You don't get upset over guys like Chris – you just have great sex.'

'Yeah?! *Really*?!' I realize this may sound over-eager so I check myself. 'Oh, really. That's good.'

'What d'you mean, *good*?'

'Oh, just... good that you can talk about it openly now.'

Sasha looks at me suspiciously but doesn't say anything.

Party party

'Party's off!' Rob says, and we all yell in protest.

'It can't be!' I say. 'We've got all these balloons blown up! Sooz has made a cake.'

'Can't have alcohol in the café,' he says.

We groan.

Tonight is the Welcome Home Louise party. She's been off college getting her leg fixed – she broke something when she fell through the window at the pool. We all feel a bit guilty about her – hence the party. I mean, if we hadn't been hiding from her she wouldn't have followed us and fallen through the window.

'I've got an idea,' I say to the others. 'I bet Chris would help us out. His mate's doing a set tonight at the bar – we could have the party there.'

'No!' Rob says, straight away. 'We're not asking him.'

'Why not?' I say. 'He's ancient history! Only this morning Sasha was saying how she was over him.'

'What?' Rob says sharply.

'Thanks, Nicki,' Sasha says under her breath.

'Look,' I say, 'I hate Chris as much as the next person, but if this party really is for Limpet then we ought to put personal differences aside and get it sorted.'

Everyone thinks about this.

'As much as I hate to admit it, she's right,' Sooz says, and in the end they all agree.

I'm saying *Yeah*! to myself, but not looking as if I am.

I can't stop thinking about what I could get up to with Chris.

Hook that guy (Tip 13)

Play hard to get. An oldie, but a goodie.

While Rob hangs back, glowering at anything that moves, Sooz and Sasha make party arrangements with Chris. I pretend to read a magazine, feigning indifference, but actually so aware of Chris that all the hairs on the back of my neck are standing up. What is it about this guy that so gets to me?

Well, I guess I know. He's pure sex.

S-e-x.

'Do we owe you anything?' Sasha asks him when they've got everything fixed.

'No, pleased to help you out. Make sure you all behave yourselves...' He turns to me, whips away my magazine. It's only then that I realize I've been reading it upside down. 'Especially *you*,' he adds.

A look flashes between us.

As I said: pure sex.

Plan A

This thing between us – this niggly, bickering, edgy relationship – has got to be resolved one way or the other.

Tonight, it's shit or bust.

Chris won't know what's hit him.

Plan B

'Call for me later,' I say to Jamie. 'We can go for a drink or something. Liven the night up a bit.'

'What?' he says, staggered. 'Call? For you?'

I shrug and pretend not to notice that the poor lamb is quite overcome. 'Yeah. Haven't made other plans, have you?'

'N... no.'

'Good. Around seven?'

'It's a date,' Jamie says eagerly.

Jamie

I'm not really taking advantage. I know Jamie fancies me – he's made that obvious – so I'm just spreading my charms a bit.

Mum and Dad are out. Not together – they don't do 'together' any more. In fact, they've even stopped rowing.

This, I know, is a bad sign.

However, they're out and that's good.

Jamie arrives dead on seven and I'm still in my robe. This isn't calculated. I've just taken a long time to get ready.

Who knows what bits of me are going to be on show later...?

I've left a bottle of wine on the side and Jamie pours us a glass each. He's nervous and I do my best to make him feel at ease, telling him that white wine makes me tipsy. His eyes nearly pop out of his head when I change my top and ask him to do it up for me.

There's something about Jamie. It's like... unconditional

love. Whatever I do, he still fancies me. I don't even have to try very hard.

Before we leave I give him a quick kiss. As a reward for being so cute. It hints of the treats in store if he gets lucky.

And if Plan A doesn't work.

Chris

The bar's really crowded but Chris and I spot each other straight away.

Our eyes lock.

As I wriggle past, Chris grabs me and whispers in my ear, 'Jamie's not your type.'

'Jealous?' I ask.

'Ha ha. Yeah, right,' Chris says. He just turns away, and a blonde girl of about twenty falls into his arms. 'Cassie!' he says. 'Haven't seen you for ages.'

I turn my back on him and say hello to all the others. Across one wall, they've put up a big banner saying *Welcome back, Louise*.

'Looks OK!' I say. 'Not nearly as tacky as I thought it would.'

'Well, thanks for your help,' says Sooz sarcastically.

She walks off and the next minute she's deep in conversation with Jamie. I know it's about me because she's giving me the evil eye while she mouths off.

Why can't she keep her sticky beak out of things?

Jamie

'What's with you and Jamie?' Sasha asks me later in the loo.

I shrug. 'I like him.'

'In what sense are we talking here?'

'He's kind. Funny.'

'So... you're making a move on him?'

I fluff my hair up a little more in the mirror.

'I've made it!' I say flippantly.

'You kissed him?'

I laugh. 'Just a peck.' I lower my voice slightly. 'He's just my Plan B, so I'm not going to too much effort.'

'So, who's A?'

'Well...' I hesitate and don't know whether to tell her or not, but I've had a few drinks by now so I'm in the mood for confessions. 'Don't go off on me, but I sense this incredible chemistry with Chris.'

Her jaw drops. 'No!'

'It doesn't bother you, does it?'

'It's not that. I can't tell you who to go for. Just be careful, all right?'

'I can handle Chris,' I say rather airily. 'You said yourself – you've got to use these guys, play them at their own game.'

'Yeah, but what if he's not interested in you, Nicki?'

'Then it's back to Plan B. Jamie's lucky night.'

Sasha grins at me as she goes out. 'You're priceless, d'you know that?'

I decide to change my hairstyle slightly and move back to the mirror. As I do so, Sooz emerges from one of the cubicles.

My heart misses a beat and then I think – so what?

Sooz

'Don't play with Jamie!' she says.

'Nice little eavesdrop?' I ask coolly.

'You know he likes you. Why d'you have to mess him around?'

'If you fancy Jamie, just tell me and I'll back off.' I raise one eyebrow. 'Or is it *me* you're interested in?'

'Don't flatter yourself!'

'Don't worry, Sooz, I won't tell anyone!' I say, and I plant a smacker on her cheek and leave the loo, giggling.

Jamie

Jamie and I dance, up close and personal. Of course, he doesn't know it, but I'm doing it as much for the delectation of Chris – nearby with the Cassie person – as I am for him.

Two for the price of one...

Cruella de Ville comes up, still angry from our encounter in the loo, and tries to warn Jamie off me. I let her have her moment with him and take the opportunity to go up to the bar.

Chris

I order a drink and he's there immediately, telling the barman to put it on his tab.

'Think you're pretty smooth, don't you?' I say.

'I know I am.'

'And way too sure of yourself.'

Chris looks me over. 'Stop singing my praises or I'm gonna think you want to get my trousers off.'

He must be psychic. I feel an electric charge run through me. But I don't let on. 'I don't like you, remember?'

'Oh yeah. And I don't like you, either.'

We smile at each other suggestively and I can actually feel my temperature rising... and then Jamie appears.

He is so not welcome.

He offers to get us a drink and we show our full glasses.

He asks me if I'm coming back to dance and I shake my head. 'Chris is going to give me a behind-the-scenes tour,' I say.

Chris just looks at me – a look that turns my insides to liquid – and I take his arm. We walk off, leaving Jamie looking devastated.

Sad, really. He didn't know he was only Plan B.

The store cupboard

We only make it as far as a deep walk-in cupboard. Chris kicks the door shut then works fast and furiously and I hardly know what's hit me. Not only does the earth move but all the stuff on the shelves moves too, and I'm not sure what's happening or where I am.

And then – moments later – it's over. Chris is standing up and rearranging his clothes.

I feel all shaky and strange. Is that going to be it?

A quickie in a cupboard?

For some unaccountable reason I want more. I want to hold onto Chris, make something more of what we've just had. But he's tidying himself, brushing himself down, smoothing out the creases on his trousers.

He says, 'I hate it when people try to make something more than it is, you know.'

'Oh me too,' I agree quickly. 'Absolutely.'

'Girls who get all clingy.'

'Yeah. Want you to hold them...'

'Whisper sweet nothings!' Chris says in a jeering tone.

'Call you up all the time... buy you those little chocolate hearts...' I stop, realizing that I'm describing those guys – Toby Jarvis for one – that I've ditched so easily.

'We have an understanding, yeah?'

''Course!' I say breezily.

'We don't have to pretend we want more than we just had...'

'Cool,' I say.

But I am – oh, *devastated...*

The brush-off

I take some deep breaths, check my appearance out in the loo, and go back into the bar.

Chris is chatting to Cassie.

I plaster a smile on my face and go up to them. 'Chris...?'

He turns. He looks at me coldly, not at all as if we'd just had a steamy session. 'I'll speak to you later, yeah.'

As I stare at him, stunned, he puts an arm around Cassie and leads her off. He's talking to her, whispering suggestively. He doesn't even glance back at me.

I can't quite believe this.

Sooz comes up, puts an arm around me. I know from the look on her face that she's seen everything.

'What goes around comes around, eh?' she says, and she gives me a plonking kiss on the cheek.

I push her off and walk away. I have to get out, get away from everyone...

I head for the loo and once in there I lean over the sink, feeling sick. I begin to cry and Sasha comes in.

'He used me, Sash!' I sob. 'Chris used me and went off with that blonde.'

'Don't, girl! He's not worth it,' she says, stroking my arm. 'Come on, wash your face. I'm not going to let you cry over him.'

'I can't believe I was so stupid. I threw myself at him!'

'Well, at least you didn't sleep with him,' Sasha says comfortingly.

I am silent.

She looks at me closely. 'Oh my God, Nicki! When? Where?'

I shake my head. I can't tell her; I'm too ashamed. Fancy doing it in a store cupboard...

'I am so low,' I say brokenly. 'So easy and so low.'

'Don't say that! He's a very persuasive bloke. I should know,' Sasha says.

I realize I've been played at my own game. 'I was just his B plan!' I say.

Sasha says quietly, 'Maybe you should spare a thought for Jamie, then.'

This really pulls me up short. What Chris has done to me, I've already done to countless guys before. Worst of all, I've done it to Jamie, too. And Jamie is supposed to be my friend...

Sorry

Sasha goes out and I lock myself in a cubicle and just sit there for a few moments, thinking deeply. I'll sort out my feelings for Chris later. But right now I have to sort out Jamie.

Back outside I go straight up to him. I say I'm really sorry, that I've led him on all night and I shouldn't have done.

Jamie, bless him, beams at me. 'That's OK,' he says. 'I don't mind.'

'No,' I protest. 'You're a great guy. I shouldn't mess with your feelings.'

'Has Sooz been on at you?'

'It's nothing to do with Sooz. It's me. Forgive me?'

Jamie looks at me. He's got that puppy-dog look in his eyes. 'If you snog me, maybe.'

'Jamie!'

'I'm serious. One snog. A proper one.'

'You realize what I've been saying. It won't mean anything!'

'Meaningless is fine.'

I kiss him and it's soft and tender and all the things I didn't get from Chris's kisses. I'm just really getting into it when suddenly, violently, we are torn apart.

'You have no morals!' Sooz screams at me.

Jamie tells her to get lost.

She grabs me again. 'Jamie's got feelings, you know.'

'Shut it, Sooz. You've got this all wrong,' Jamie says.

'No. You've got it wrong. She's just had sex with Chris!'

I look at her incredulously. 'Oh, tell the whole world, why don't you?'

'You're such a slapper!' Sooz says.

I snap at this. 'And you are a twisted little virgin who hates the thought of anyone else having any fun.'

She looks shocked at this, turns away – and then turns back suddenly and punches me one. Hard.

I'm not going to let her get away with this. I launch myself onto her and we end up on the floor, kicking and fighting.

Tables and chairs go flying, people yell at us and clap and things get smashed – including Limpet's Welcome Home cake.

In the midst of all this, the girl herself appears. 'Oh... er... hi, Louise,' I say, removing my elbow from a mess of cream and icing sugar. 'Glad you're back.'

Limpet

The bar is cleared up, breakages have been dealt with and nearly everyone's gone. Limpet and I are sitting contemplating the remains of the cake.

I pop a bit in my mouth. 'It still tastes okay,' I say to her. 'Want to try some?'

She shakes her head. 'No, that's all right.'

'I'm sorry we messed up the party.'

'Don't worry. It's the thought that counts,' she says.

That girl is such a cliché.

I'm listening to her, but I'm also trying to listen to Jamie, who's blowing up Sooz some. I hear her saying she thought they were friends. Then I hear him say that he's sick of listening to her and her hang-ups. That she should get some help.

He walks off.

He's quite right about the help. Someone ought to tell Sooz that she's a nosy, scheming bitch and we're not prepared to have her around if she carries on like that.

'What was the fight about, anyway?' Limpet asks me.

I shake my head. 'I haven't a clue. She's got a screw loose, if you ask me.'

Ouch!

The next day I wake up with an almighty black eye. It's just as well I'm not going out with Chris again, I think.

And then I sigh a bit.

Zsa-Zsa revisited

Alex takes me to a gay club.

I love it. The men are so much sexier, more colourful, funnier.

Funniest of all is a guy we're sitting next to. He's gay in a camp, *Are You Being Served?* sort of way, not in an Alex way. I know I've seen him before but I can't think where. Then he tells me he works in Zsa-Zsa.

'Of course!' I say. 'I love it in there.'

'Exotic garments from around the world,' he says. '*And* in extra large sizes.'

'For fat people?'

'For gay men! Some of us do like a little touch of frou-frou about our parts.'

He says he's seen me in the shop. 'I think you got something from us recently, didn't you?'

I'm wearing the thong and — by God, he can't possibly

know I've pinched it, can he? – it suddenly goes all tight and scratchy.

'Something in red, perhaps?' He raises his eyebrows and I'm *convinced* he knows.

Maybe I was seen.

Why didn't they come after me? Arrest me on the spot?

Maybe they lost me in the shopping crowd. Maybe they're waiting until I go past the shop again, and then they'll rush out and get me.

I'm worried. I confide in Alex but he says he wants nothing to do with it.

'It's not that I mind being taken in hand by the police,' he tells me. 'But it would have to be Dan doing it.' He nudges me. 'Geddit? Dan... taking me in hand.'

'Yeah, yeah,' I say. I persuade him to come home with me, though, and I get some cash and an envelope and then we go into town.

I write on the envelope: *Cash enclosed for item taken in error.*

And then I put it through their door.

Of course, wearing it won't be the same now it's paid for.

Fight

It was not my fault.

'It so wasn't,' I say to the others.

It was all down to Sooz. That girl could win a prize for best bitch in the show.

And – oh, maybe it was a bit of Chris's fault, too.

We were at Rob and Sasha's. Jamie had persuaded them to have a party so that he could come on strong to this new girl of his. But she turned up with six or so heavyweights, so Jamie was out of the running with her before he'd even started.

As for me – well, I had the rats with Chris. I'd been thinking about him a lot since the cupboard encounter and was trying to convince myself that he'd only gone off with the blonde to make me jealous – that he still fancied me as much as I fancied him...

So when I arrived at the party and Chris looked pleased to see me (and groped my bum) I thought that he and I might be on again.

The trouble was, Chris went off to chat to Alex. And *stayed* chatting to Alex.

Now, I've nothing against gay men, but when they monopolize the only love god for miles around, it gets to you a bit.

So I went over and told Alex that his boyfriend was looking for him. And I kind of inferred that Chris and Alex had something going on between them.

Alex said quite crossly, 'You know, Nicki – the difference between you and me is that I can actually talk to a bloke and not want to get into his trousers.'

Behind me, I heard Sooz laughing.

'So why are you two always going off together, then?' I asked Alex.

Chris told me to chill out. Said they'd got things to discuss.

The bitch laughed at me again. I went up and asked her what was so funny.

'I just find it amusing,' she said. 'You know – Chris isn't interested in you, so he's got to be gay.'

I lost it with her. 'Just get out of my face, Sooz!' I shouted, and when Alex stepped in to try to make the peace I pushed him out of the way. He blundered into some bloke who elbowed him in the face.

Suddenly it went all *Reservoir Dogs*: people were rolling round the floor and half the flat went flying through the air.

Oops

We are now contemplating the resulting mess.

'You pushed me, Tinkerbell,' Sooz is saying. 'That started all this.'

'You're pathetic!' I say. 'Everyone knows you're incredibly jealous of me.'

'Yeah, Nicki. You're my role model.'

'At least I'm not some kind of freak!' I say.

Sasha suddenly shouts, 'Enough!'

She looks as if she's going to burst into tears. 'I've had enough, OK?' she says. 'We're meant to be looking after this place, not trashing it. Just all go, right!'

I try to say sorry but she cuts me off.

I go home.

I am so fed up.

Chris. Well, he obviously couldn't give a shit about me.

But to me it's unfinished business. It hurts.

I can't stop thinking about him and wondering if he's thinking of me.

I know he's not.

I look around me: there's someone in a boiled-egg swimming hat doing a very slow breaststroke in the pool, two kids picking ants out of the cracked tiles and Mum asleep on a sunbed with her mouth open.

It is *so* boring here.

No decent waiters.

No lads on stag weekends.

And the tour rep – how's this for bad luck? – is a girl.

There isn't a sign or a sniff of a holiday romance and all I can think about is what the gang are getting up to at home without me.

Mum keeps trying to talk to me about the divorce (yeah, it's come to that), referring all the time to 'your father', like he's some alien person who's nothing to do with her. But I don't want to know. Let them sort it out for themselves; I'm not going to take sides. When she's not trying to have Meaningful Talks she just dozes around reading crappy romance novels or swigging funny-coloured drinks.

There's just nothing to do. I haven't even brought any of my set books with me. We left in such a hurry that I only had time to throw a couple of bikinis and a handful of T-shirts in a bag, and we were off.

I yawn. It's OK here – the sun and everything – but I want action.

Guy action.

And I want it now...

I frown at Mum, who's starting to snore gently, and make her roll over onto her stomach so no one can see her fillings. I then go upstairs to our room and put on my tightest,

Dear Sasha,

First of all — big sorries for the mess-up at the party. It really wasn't my fault — that snout-face Sooz started it all by slagging me off in front of everyone. Anyway, I hope Jamie cleared the place up for you OK.

Guess you'll be surprised to get this! My mum found a credit card of my dad's (the only one he hadn't stopped) and booked us up at the last minute, so we're out here for three weeks working on our tans and checking out the waiters.

More news as it happens. Write back.
Lots of love, Nicki.

shortest shorts, a bright green strappy top and a pair of high-heeled mules. I leave a note for Mum saying I've gone shopping (if she wakes up and I'm not there she'll have the pool dragged) and walk down the hill towards the town.

First the bars.

I do a circuit without much luck. Either the bars are owned by guys who've come out from Essex to make good, or they're

being run by the oh-so-obvious Spanish guys with slicked-back hair and tight trousers – the ones who call out, 'I lurve you!' to every vaguely English-looking girl who passes.

I can do better than them, I think.

Or can I?

Because I trawl the bars without chancing on anyone even halfway fanciable.

I can't believe it: sun, sand, sea and... that vital last word is missing.

When, reluctantly, I go back to the hotel, Mum is chatting to a woman with two small children. I wave to tell her I'm back, then stay on the other side of the pool, well away from them. I do not intend to get lumbered with looking after those children.

I strip off and start sunbathing, and – almost asleep –

Hi, Jamie,

Well, here I am wearing very little and getting my leg over a sunbed. Wish you were here! I've been thinking about our snog. It was good! I've been thinking about you, too, and – not being big-headed, but I know you've had a bit of a thing about me – wondering about us taking things further. It's difficult to write much on a postcard but I guess you'll know what I mean. How about it?

All my love, Nicki
(knickerless Nicki at the moment!)

have a funny little daydream about Jamie and the snog we had. I know, positively, that something is going to happen between us two sooner or later, and if I don't meet anyone on this holiday it's more likely to be sooner. Maybe he'll meet me at the airport...

I'm wondering who else to send a postcard to. Sooz? Just to (rather generously) try to put everything right between us?

Maybe.

Mum wants me to pop down to the shop and get an English newspaper for her.

I find this sort of behaviour so embarrassing — she'll be requesting fish and chips instead of paella next — but I agree to go so that I can post the card to Jamie. On the way, I have a pleasant five minutes imagining what he'll do when he gets it...

I buy a batch of stamps in the newspaper shop. The woman who serves me is a typical old Spanish lady with a long black dress and skin like a walnut. I hand over a note. She seems to have run out of change, so calls for someone from the back room.

He comes.

Oh, wow!

His name is Freddie. Which doesn't sound very Spanish, but is when you say it with a sexy accent. He has smooth olive skin, thick dark hair and the most beautiful chestnut-brown eyes I've ever seen.

I look at him and practically go into a swoon.

He takes my hand and counts the coins into it. As he does so he looks into my eyes and I stutter and shake and forget my few words of Spanish.

'You stay here? In our town?' he asks.

'Yes... I... with my mother at the Hotel Splendide...' I gabble. And then something else takes over.

Hook that guy (Tip 14)

I deliberately make myself go pink. I can! This signals to a guy that you are deeply attracted. And then I open my lips and pout, just a little...

It obviously works, because you know those movies where the couple only have to look at each other to start ripping off their clothes? Well, I swear that if we hadn't been in the middle of a shop with his old mum standing by, we'd have had a sensational time right there and then on the wooden floor.

The magnetism... chemistry... between us is just *amazing*.

We break our looks at last and he – Freddie – stands in the doorway and stares at me all the way back up the street. I post the card to Jamie and go back to the hotel to take a cold shower.

Hi Sasha,
Thanks for yours. I can't believe it about
Sooz and Jamie! Are you really sure they
ended up together after your party? What's
the matter with the guy? Is he having a crisis?
The annoying thing is, I've just written to him
practically offering myself on a plate!
Now I feel utterly stupid.

Anyway, sod all that because I've just
met the most wonderful Spanish guy, name
of Freddie. He works in the newsagents' —
well, he probably owns it — and I have fallen
madly in lust.   More soon,

Lots of love, Nicki

Dear Jamie,
I hope you won't get the wrong idea from my
last card! Now I've thought about it a bit
more I know it wouldn't really work between
us two. It would just end up with you getting
hurt.

So let's just stay best of friends. That
way, we'll never have to say goodbye.

Lots of love, Nicki

It's the following afternoon and I'm offering to go and get Mum a newspaper.

'I don't think I'll have one today,' she says. 'It's just the same old stuff.'

I get up. 'You can give me the money when I get back,' I say.

'I said I didn't want one...' she says crossly, but I pretend not to hear her.

I drift down the hill into town. He's there, outside the shop. I'm sure he's been waiting for me.

I buy a paper and then we sit down on two little stools outside the shop and talk. He speaks very good English – he's been learning it since he was six.

nicki's secrets

He has the most hypnotizing come-to-bed eyes and as I stare into them I'm so overcome that I keep forgetting what I'm saying.

He asks if I have a boyfriend at home. I say I haven't, and I sort of imply that I do not have boyfriends. That my parents are very strict and that I am virtuous.

Dearest Sasha,

I am mad about the Freddie that I told you about. I have been down to his shop twice more and we've had sexy conversations, and tonight I'm meeting him on the beach.
Can't wait! When it happens it will be simply wonderful...

I may stay out here permanently.
Lots of love,

Nicki
PS Any more news on Jamie and Sooz?

I think this is better.

He says he'd like to come to England, that there are more opportunities there. Hesitatingly, he asks if he may tell me that I have a beautiful body. It's the first time I've heard someone say that without them adding, '... *will you hold it against me*?'

I blush to order.

I let him make all the running and feel I am acting out some beautiful old-age seduction scene. I know, just know, he's as besotted with me as I am with him.

He asks me if I can meet him later when the shop is closed.

I hesitate, look down, say in a small voice that I cannot resist him.

After dinner, I tell Mum I'm going down to the village to help a Spanish boy improve his English and I may be some time.

I meet Freddie and as we walk hand in hand along the beach, past the little fishing boats and rows of whitewashed cottages, it's like we're in a wonderful dream. The sun sets, turning the sky tangerine and purple, and we talk and laugh and splash in little waves at the edge of the water. I drop my shoes somewhere along the way and don't care.

We talk of everything.

He asks if I believe in love at first sight and I say I never have done before...

He asks me how many days I have left, and we draw them out in the sand and talk about what we'll do on each one of them.

He says he'll be coming to England soon. Very soon.

I ask why he can't come now. Come back with me.

He says brokenly, looking abashed, that ages ago – years ago – his dying grandmother made him promise to marry the daughter of a friend. They have never loved each other, but he did as the old lady wished.

'You're married!?' I gasp.

'Only in name,' he says quickly. 'It has never been... how you say... we have never done the sexual act.'

'So you don't live together?'

'I have not seen her for two years. We do not even speak... but I must to have the marriage annulled before I can come to England. When the marriage ends the shop can be sold.'

'Oh,' I say.

'But it is very expensive to live in England. Unless I could find somewhere cheap to stay until my annulment comes through.'

He strokes the back of my neck and I look up into his liquid brown eyes. 'I may be able to help you...' I say.

He clasps me to him, we start kissing and then we sink gently onto the ground.

It's a beautiful moment and a classic setting: golden sand, scarlet sunset, waves lapping at our feet – a beautiful young virgin being swept away by passion with a man she truly loves.

I'm a *wonderful* actress...

I go back to the hotel in the small hours, utterly in love.

Darling Sasha,

I can never come back!

At least, I can never come back without him.

I am ridiculously much in love.

Your besotted best friend,

Nicki.

I tell Mum about Freddie. She says, 'You'll get over it, darling. It's a holiday romance, that's all.'

It so isn't.

Freddie and I meet again. We go for a meal together but I am so choked with love that I can't swallow anything. We drink a little champagne and a gypsy violinist comes round to our

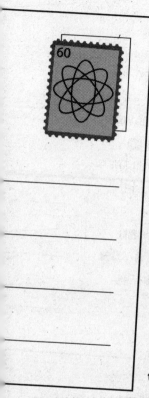

table and begins to serenade us. Freddie translates: he is singing a song about love between two people from different backgrounds, like Romeo and Juliet, who find a way to be together despite all the odds.

It's amazing that the gypsy violinist knows all this.

We talk about what we'll do when Freddie comes to London. He says he'll have money from the sale of the shop very soon, and when he gets that he'll buy a shop of his own. I ask what sort (florists? shoes? fashion boutique?) and he says it will probably be one selling newspapers, because that's the trade he knows.

This doesn't sound so good to me, but I don't say anything. Time enough when he arrives to talk him round to a gorgeous little lingerie shop off the Fulham Road.

We arrange to meet the next day.

I only have two more days left! I will probably expire of love without him.

Dear Sooz,

I think we both ought to try, before next term starts, to put things right between us.

I know we both have very different views on life but this holiday has made me see things in a new way. I am so madly in love with someone I've met out here that I feel I love the whole world.

I just want to wish you, honestly and truly, every happiness in whatever it is you're doing (or whoever you're going out with!)

Love from Nicki

I'm waiting outside the hotel. Freddie promised to come for me at six o'clock.

He's late. I look at my watch for the millionth time and it's nearly seven!

I can't believe he's stood me up. There must be something wrong.

Badly wrong.

He's had an accident, perhaps.

He's lying injured at the side of the road.

I leave a message at Reception and walk down into the town towards his shop. I've spoken to his mother several times (though she's not what you'd call friendly) and I know his family live in a flat above it.

I tell myself not to feel so anxious. It doesn't have to be an accident – maybe he's just had to work late and has lost the tele-phone number of the hotel.

There are a number of people hanging about outside the shop and I'm just about to cross the road and go in when he – Freddie – comes out.

I hesitate... because he's got a girl with him.

A Spanish girl.

And she's very pregnant.

I slink back in the doorway of the shop opposite, staring and wondering. It's his sister, maybe. Or his cousin. They have big extended families over here and are very close.

He helps the girl into a car at the kerb. And then he bends over her and kisses her tenderly on the lips. He puts his hand on her bump and pats it and she laughs. She says something and looks at her watch. He nods.

Dear Sasha,

It's all over between me and Freddie.
I thought I'd be devastated but well, I guess these things happen. Holiday romances — they blow up like a summer storm and can be over just as quickly. The important thing is just to live through them.
I guess our love was too beautiful to be real, too precious to survive in this world.
I'll tell you all about it when I get back and show you the photos.

Lots of love, Nicki

And then she's driving off and he's waving and blowing kisses.

It is not his sister or his cousin.

I stay hidden in the doorway. I want to see what he's going to do.

What he does is look at his watch again, shout something to a person in the shop, then start running up the road towards my hotel.

Except, of course, I'm not there.

Hasn't seen his wife for two years, eh? Well, he obviously writes very passionate letters.

Riggs

I have met THE most gorgeous man.

Man.

Not boy.

He's the sort of man who could take me places. He's a music producer. He dresses immaculately, has money to set alight and knows just where he's going in the world. He's also fantastically, hornily sexy.

We met at the type of place I just don't go to enough: the smartest restaurant on the Thames, at a press launch. Amid the champagne and fireworks, there he was across a smoky room: sending out signals, smiling at me, leading me on...

The trouble is, he hasn't returned my calls.

This doesn't mean he doesn't fancy me – just that he's overworked. And I know from experience that if you want to hook this type, you've got to make the running yourself.

So I've staked out the place where he works and I'm waiting for him to turn up.

Then he's going to get the full benefit of my considerable ability to turn men on.

Just as I'm checking my mobile for messages – maybe he's phoned since I came out? – I see a taxi pull up on the other side of the road.

Setting the bait

Riggs gets out of the taxi and I'm up and outta there like a flash – almost knocking over Sasha, who's coming back with the coffees.

Did I mention we're in a café opposite his recording studios?

'Nicki!' she yells after me, but I don't stop.

I catch him just as he's about to go through the swing doors.

'Riggs!'

He turns, surprised. And pleased, I think.

'This is so like fate... I was just across the road!' I say. 'I had no idea you worked round here.' I sound genuine. I really *should* be an actress.

He pays the driver and looks at me, slightly bemused.

'It's Nicki. From the party a couple of nights back?'

He remembers me. Of course he remembers me.

'I'm not sure if you got my messages...'

'Yeah, I did, actually,' he says. 'I've just been...'

'Because I realized afterwards that I hadn't explained myself properly,' I gabble. 'I'm doing a piece on the music industry for our college magazine and I wondered if you'd mind having a quick chat about it.'

He looks at his watch.

'A couple of minutes should do it. I know how terrifically busy you are.'

I have new – fur – eyelashes. I do the two-eye wink and smile up at him. 'Really. You'd be doing me such a good turn if you could possibly just spare a moment...'

He takes the bait.

Spinning the line

We're in his studio and he's at a mixing desk. I want to stop and take it all in so I can tell Sasha about it, but I'm trying to be the sophisticated reporter.

I'm asking him questions, but they're double-edged.

So when I ask: *'What would be your advice to anyone wanting to break into the music industry?'* what I'm actually saying is, *'What would be your advice to anyone trying to seduce you?'*

He answers: 'You've got to be persistent, for one thing. You've got to be passionate. And you've got to really know what you like.'

I nod.

Most certainly a yes to all three.

We start to chat more generally and I'm thinking wow, we're really making a connection here, but then he looks at his watch.

'Time's up,' he says.

Hook that guy (Tip 15)

As you say goodbye, bend over slightly so that he notices your cleavage. A perfumed sachet tucked in your bra will ensure that at least two of his senses are engaged.

Miscasting

Riggs sees me back to the reception area. Much to my annoyance (she's looking fairly stunning), Sasha has got fed up sitting in the café and has come over to wait for me.

Riggs thinks she's waiting for him. He says, 'You my four-thirty?'

Sasha says no, she's with me.

'Pity,' Riggs says.

I don't like the way he's looking at her.

But it doesn't mean anything. Just that he's a guy who appreciates a good-looking woman. And what's wrong with that? Besides, she's not going to respond, is she? She loves Rob for ever and ever amen.

Catch!

Just as we've left the building he comes out after us holding a flyer for a gig.

'You and your mate might like to come to this on Wednesday.'

'Sure!' I say eagerly.

'I'll put you both down at the door, yeah?'

I smile to myself.

Old, young, rich... I've never known my pulling techniques to fail.

Meantime...

I am so delighted with getting what is almost a date with Riggs that I am not even slightly annoyed that Jamie and Sooz do seem to have something – something as yet unspecified – going on. Jamie is sweet but he's such small fry. And if he prefers someone as bizarre as Sooz to me – well, I guess he is just going to get what he deserves.

The gig

Things are going OK. OKish. But only ish, because Riggs is a whole different animal to the type I usually go out with.

Such a big catch.

He's working the room but he comes over to me and Sasha to ask us what we think about the music.

I say I think it's amazing. 'The ambiance... the band is brilliant. I really rate it here,' I say gushily.

'But you don't?' Riggs is looking at Sasha hard.

'Sasha's not into this stuff,' I say quickly. 'Not her sort of music. She's got decks at home – she mixes, you know.' I laugh as if it's the craziest thing I've ever heard. 'She mixes all these little tapes for herself!'

But Riggs isn't laughing, he's looking interested. 'You should send me a demo tape,' he says. 'We're always looking for new talent.'

'I don't think I'm your kind of thing,' Sasha says.

'Don't be too sure,' says Riggs. And you can call me paranoid if you want, but it looks to me as if he's flirting with her. I'm like – what's going on? Look at me, over here, I'm the one you want!

I think to myself that drastic times call for drastic measures. And anyway, he's wasting his time with Sasha 'cos she's so into

Rob. I put my hand on his arm and look at him from under my eyelashes, then I toss my head and flick my hair away from my face. It falls back, heavy and silky, over my cheeks.

I'm about to come out with something so loaded (and filthy) that it'll make his eyes come out on stalks, when I hear a roar from across the dance floor of 'Nickeee! Sashaaaa!' and a sloppily drunk Jamie and Alex lurch across the room towards us.

I am *so* embarrassed.

'How did you two get in?' I ask.

'There's three of us – Sooz is here an' all! We blagged our way in!' says Alex.

Jamie, doing his impression of a Cheshire cat, says, 'Told them on the door we were friends of Riggs, didn't we?'

'Hang on, I...'

'That's the bloke you were going on about, wasn't it?' Jamie goes on, very slurred, 'The geezer who invited you?'

'Riggs 'n' me – we're like that!' Alex says, holding up two crossed fingers.

From beside me, Riggs smiles and cuts in, 'If we are, I must have missed it.'

'This is Riggs,' I say in a tight voice. 'Riggs, these are my friends, Jamie and Alex.'

'Glad you could make it,' Riggs says.

'Ooops!' says Jamie.

Sasha?

Riggs is OK about it, actually, but then I suppose when you've got that much dough you don't care about a few spongers. Jamie goes off to trail Sooz, and Alex stays with us. As I watch him chatting away to Riggs I have a sudden awful thought: maybe Riggs isn't responding to me quite as much as he could because he's gay!

God, I'd be gutted.

I put a smooth, manicured hand on Riggs' arm and he turns and smiles at me sexily. No, he's not gay.

So now I've got two of them: Sasha and Alex, to get rid of...

As if she knows what I'm thinking, Sasha turns to me. 'I'm going. Rob'll be wondering where I am.'

'Sure! Yeah, you go,' I say, trying not to sound too eager. 'You don't want him to worry about you.'

She says goodbye and goes off. Then suddenly, out of nowhere, Jamie appears looking utterly mashed. I mean, completely bladdered. He clutches his stomach and then just throws up all over the floor, right in front of me and Riggs.

I don't know where to look. Everyone round us groans and makes noises of disgust, but Jamie seems to recover almost immediately.

'Better out than in, eh, Nicks?' he says, and goes off to get a mop. Alex goes with him. Just as I'm working out what to say as an excuse for having someone like Jamie as a friend, Riggs disappears too. I mean, totally does a Lucan on me.

I look all round and then I see him talking to Sasha in the coat queue. And not just talking, either. Smouldering. The two of them are looking at each other with their tongues hanging out.

I stare.

I just can't believe this.

Sasha gives him one last, longing smile and goes out of the club. Riggs comes back and I wonder how I'm going to find out what they've been talking about.

He tells me, though. 'She's going to send me a tape,' he says. 'She's a bit of a difficult woman, that one.'

'She's missing her boyfriend,' I say quickly. 'Been together ages, they have. She really, really loves him.'

'Is that so?' Riggs says drily.

Goodbye

Bewildered, I sort of lose the plot after that. Riggs goes off to meet and greet, and as the night goes on I get more and more plastered. Before I know it there's hardly anyone left in the place and I'm being bundled into a mini-cab.

I hang onto Riggs' arm. This isn't what I planned at all, 'Aren't you coming with me?' I ask.

He shakes his head. 'No. You go home like a good girl, eh?'

A good girl, I want to say, is the last thing you'd call me if you knew me. But before I can come out with this witty remark he's slamming the cab door shut and the driver is off and away.

I know I haven't got enough cash for the cab home. I ask the driver to stop at a cashpoint and then, when we get there, disaster strikes. A message comes up on the screen which says, *'Your card has been retained – please contact your bank.'*

I stare at the screen in disbelief. My dad couldn't have put my allowance in this month! Either that or he's cancelled my card because I've spent too much on my Hook Riggs clothes.

The idiot! How could he do this to me?

I punch my dad's number into my mobile and when his answerphone kicks in I yell, 'Thanks for not paying my allowance into my bank this month. Because of you, I'm stranded at the Blue Room at four o'clock in the morning! How the bloody hell do you expect me to get home?'

I then trip over, break the heel on my new shoes and burst into tears. I realize that, although it'll kill me to have to do it, I have no option but to go back to the club.

Hello again

When I stumble into the Blue Room, Riggs doesn't exactly look thrilled to see me. 'I meant what I said about going home, you know,' he says. 'I've a daughter not much younger than you.'

'Look, I'm sorry,' I say. 'The machine swallowed my card and I haven't got any money for the cab.' I'm desperately trying not to cry again. I feel – and look – a right mess. Not Lolita so much as Llama.

He seems to melt a little. He takes two tenners from a wad in his pocket and hands them over. 'I'll call you another cab,' he says. 'D'you want a coffee while you wait?'

I'm just debating to myself whether I can possibly salvage something from the night when I hear a cough behind me. 'OK, Princess?' my dad's voice says, and my heart sinks.

I introduce them. Riggs is welcoming, expansive. 'Kids, eh?' he says to Dad, and they have coffee and a laugh at my expense. Dad tells him about something nauseating I did when I was two and I think, just bury me now, dead or alive...

Eventually Dad takes me home in his car and I sit in moody silence all the way. He draws up outside the house but doesn't come in, of course – Mum has banned him.

'Why did my credit card disappear?' I ask. 'What's happened at the bank?'

He looks a bit uneasy. 'Some admin error, I expect,' he says. 'I'll get it put right tomorrow.'

I look at him suspiciously.

'That Riggs bloke – he's too old for you,' he says.

'I'll decide that,' I say stiffly.

'There'll be lots of blokes, Nicks,' Dad says, taking my arm. 'You've got all that to come.'

Ha! The words *more blokes* and *hot dinners* come to mind. I get out of the car and go in to bed. As I fall asleep, I have just one thing on my mind: is there anything between Riggs and Sasha?

Riggs

When I wake up late the next morning I still feel stupid – but then I reason that Riggs is not your average Joe.

I mean, with ordinary guys, if they don't fall madly in love with me by the end of the first date, there's obviously something wrong with them. And life's too short to hang around finding out what it is.

With Riggs, though – well, he's different.

The greater the effort, the greater the reward – and with a guy of his calibre it's obviously going to take a whole lot more than suggestive talk and a push-up bra to get under his skin.

But what about him and Sasha? The way they looked at each other...

Sasha

At lunchtime I meet her in the café and have it out with her. She's all big eyes and innocence.

'I tell you, there's nothing between me and Riggs!' she says.

I frown at her.

'At least, on my part there isn't,' she goes on.

I pounce. 'So you admit that he fancies you, then?'

She shakes her head. 'No! No, I don't mean that. I just mean that I don't fancy him. I don't know what his agenda is.'

I know I look unconvinced.

I *am* unconvinced.

'Would I lie to you? You're my best friend!' she says.

She goes up to the bar to get coffees and smooches a bit with Rob, and while she's up there I decide that I've got to believe her about Riggs.

Got to.

Want to.

Don't.

Alex

We drink coffee and watch Alex, who's coming on strong to a cute guy we've never seen before.

When he goes out I say to Alex, 'Let me know if that guy ever goes straight, will you?'

'No chance,' Alex says rather smugly. 'Mark's a full-on poof.'

Sasha says, 'You wouldn't ever cheat on Dan now that you've finally got him back, though, would you?'

Alex looks from one to the other of us and grins.

'You have!' I say. 'You have already!'

'Might have,' Alex says airily.

I gasp, amazed. 'That's it,' I say, 'I'm resigning as head slapper of the group.'

Close call

My mobile rings and I snatch it up and look at the display. It is! It's him!

I turn away from everyone else. I want Riggs all to myself.

'Hi, Riggs!' I say, and I'm, like, practically gabbling. I tell myself to calm down. 'I'm really pleased you rang. I was going to get in touch to apologize for my dad and all that stuff last night and I wondered if...'

'Can't stop now, sweetheart, I'm in traffic. I'm ringing to ask for your friend's number. She dropped in a tape and I want to talk to her about it.'

I am gutted.

I mean *gutted*.

But I give him Sasha's number. What else can I do?

Last supper

That evening, for some reason, Sasha and Rob invite me round for a meal. I go – mostly so I can try and convince myself that they're still Mr and Mrs Cosy and that there is nothing at all between her and Riggs.

I haven't said anything about the phone call. I want to see if she mentions it first. She doesn't, so while she's giving the finishing touches to the pasta I say, dead casual, 'Oh, forgot to say. Did Riggs ring you? He asked me for your number.'

'Oh yeah!' She turns those big innocent eyes on me. 'I forgot to say too. He rang to say he's already listened to my tape. He likes it.'

'You didn't tell me you'd taken a tape in.'

She shrugs. Rob is in the other room but she lowers her voice anyway. 'Don't get hung up on this, Nicki. Riggs means nothing to me – except, maybe, as a way of getting a break in the music world. You know I love Rob. I only want to be with him.'

'Mmm,' I say.

'But while we're on the subject, hon' – he's not right for you.'

'Who says?' I ask indignantly.

'I do. And I say you're going to make a fool of yourself if you carry on chasing him.'

I'm fairly annoyed at this. 'Well, thank you, Oprah,' I say. 'If I need any more advice I'll ask for it.'

'Don't be like that, Nicki!'

But I'm collecting my jacket by now. Heading out of the door. Behind me I hear Rob say, 'What's up with her?' but I don't wait to hear what excuse she gives.

I go home to brood.

A date

The next day I'm sitting in the café opposite the recording studios where Riggs works.

So? They do a really great machiato here.

And, well – suffering helps the soul, they say. I mean, not too much suffering or it tells on the complexion, but just a little suffering makes a girl more interesting.

I have to say goodbye to him in my head.

Move on.

Just as I'm thinking that, Riggs strides out of the studios, looking kinda gorgeous, and before I can stop myself I'm up and following him down the road.

He stops outside a swish Italian restaurant, glances at his watch, and goes inside.

I am intrigued.

I am curious.

I am just plain nosy.

He goes up to a girl already seated at a table. She's behind a pillar and I don't see her face at first, but he bends over and kisses her cheek and she puts a hand on his shoulder.

It's an intimate gesture.

Like they're very good friends. Or more.

As she leans forward, I see that the girl is Sasha.

 # Bitch

My best friend is a two-faced bitch and I'm not speaking to her.

Oh, I'm *so* not speaking to her.

When I go in the café the following day, she and Rob are snogging over the counter. Snogging! As if she really cares about him. As if she's not two-timing him with Riggs.

She comes up to me, nice as pie, and tries to pay for my coffee.

I don't let her.

She knows how mad I am about Riggs.

How *could* she?

Sasha

'I want to be totally straight with you,' she says in the college canteen the next day.

'Really?' I mutter sarcastically.

'Really,' she insists. 'We need to talk.'

She rubs her nose.

That's a sign that someone's lying, of course.

'Riggs...' she begins. 'OK, there is something between us. Some attraction or other.'

I don't speak.

'But I don't intend to take it any further. I love Rob – you know I do.'

'Loving Rob never stopped you shagging Chris.'

'That was different,' she says. 'Riggs is... well, he can really influence my career. With his help I can make something of myself.'

'So have you told Rob all this? Told him you're just after Riggs for his contacts? Because at the moment he's watching you like a starving man watches a piece of bread.'

'I don't see the point of telling Rob,' she says. 'I wanted to tell you, OK? You're my best friend.'

I don't say anything. Not a word.

'I don't want you to go on thinking that I'm leading Riggs

on. I don't want him to come between us.'

I look her full in the face. 'Well, thank you for your honesty,' I say.

Do I believe her?

Do I hell.

They're probably at it like rabbits.

Sooz and Jamie

We're all quite convinced that they are up to something.

Possibly... probably... doing it.

I just can't see him with Sooz, though. No way.

I wonder what it would be like to have Jamie as a boyfriend? Should I try to get him off her as a kind of experiment? No. Feel too fed up.

Can't believe that me and Riggs are no-go.

Anna

Fried breakfast in the canteen.

Not really me, but it's awful at home and I need comfort food, seeing as Mum is continually and everlastingly on the phone to solicitors/accountants/counsellors/financial consultants/Relate/solicitors again, and barely registers my presence. I wondered at first if the Relate thing meant she and Dad might get back together, but she says not.

This is it. I am the child of a broken marriage.

I'm just about to tuck in to sausage and beans when Anna comes along. She and I went to school together and used to be pretty close until she got expelled. I can't remember exactly what for, but it was something to do with the Head, a pair of tassles and a belly-button jewel.

Anna is a lot like me.

We sit down together and start chatting. Then Jamie comes by, and I can see by his reaction to her that there has been something going on between them.

I'm intrigued.

First Jamie and Sooz.

Now Jamie and Anna?

Blanked!

Sasha comes in and completely blanks me.

I can't believe this!

I leave Anna with the question mark hanging over her and go up to Sasha.

'Don't I even get a hello?' I ask.

'Oh, you've decided to talk to me now, have you?' she snaps. 'Changed your mind about me?'

I shrug. 'Forget it, then.'

'You are such a child!' Sasha retorts, and I lose it, leave my breakfast and slam out.

Dad

I don't quite know why I go to Dad's office, other than because I need to speak to someone. When I get there, there's a police car parked outside and two heavy-looking guys are speaking to him.

I wait.

At least I'm giving the workmen something to ogle as they pass by.

I think about how much easier it would be to go out with one of them. How much less complicated to have a bit of rough...

Before I can develop this novel idea any further, the policemen leave and Dad sees me waiting. But not before I've spotted how awful he looks. How worried and stressed. Is this because of the divorce, or something else?

'This is a nice surprise, Princess,' he says, trying to sound chirpy.

I nod at the departing coppers. 'What did they want?'

'Oh. Nothing. Vandals broke in again.'

I know he's lying. Why is everyone lying to me these days?

'Something on your mind, Princess?'

'Not really. Can't I just pay you a visit?'

'You can. But my guess is that there's something up.'

I suddenly feel like a child again. 'It's Sasha!' I blurt out. 'It's not fair. She's being so unreasonable! I thought we'd made it up and she just completely blanked me!'

Dad looks at me and narrows his eyes. 'Is this about a fella?'

'It's so not!' I say.

Dad holds out his arms and gives me a hug.

'She told me I was childish!' I say plaintively.

Dad laughs. 'Straight up?'

Rough

After chatting to Dad I feel a bit better, so on the way out of his hire yard I try it on with a solidly muscled bloke of about twenty.

He has very blue eyes, long hair and a tattered vest.

OK, I could do better. But I'm just keeping my hand in, right?

I smile at him and he does a double-take, startled, and then looks behind him to see if I was smiling at someone else.

Rather sweet, actually. Obviously can't believe his luck.

'Hi,' I say. I lift my eyebrows suggestively. 'You look strong.'

'Wha'?' he says. 'Do wha'?'

'You look... er... strong. Muscular.'

He looks at me completely blankly. Talk about Planet of the Apes – the guy doesn't know, can't see, that he's being chatted up.

Maybe he's foreign or something.

I put my hand out and feel his muscles. 'Big!' I say admiringly.

He doesn't react and I let my hand fall. I can't be bothered. Just can't be bothered.

To go from someone like Riggs to someone like *him* – well I'm obviously suffering from withdrawal symptoms. I cut the muscled one dead and pass on. Perhaps he'll realize later what he's missed and kill himself.

Red roses (1)

Two days later Dad is waiting for me outside college. As I head for his car, I hear Sasha calling. I look round before I've had a chance to stop myself.

She's standing there holding a bunch of long-stemmed red roses, waving at me.

I ignore her and get into Dad's car.

Dad goes over to speak to her. I can see them in the driving mirror, chatting away. Then he gets in the car and gives me the roses.

'Twelve red roses for a very special friend,' he says.

'Don't want them!'

'These things cost the earth,' he says. 'She must be really sorry.'

Grudgingly, I take them and sniff their delicate perfume. They smell divine.

'How long have you two been mates for...?'

'OK,' I say wearily.

'And you're just going to let some bloke come in and mess it all up?'

'Dad! All right, she's forgiven.'

'Tell him where to go, not her,' he says. Chance would be a fine thing, I think to myself.

Red roses (2)

'They're absolutely beautiful,' I say to Sasha in the canteen a bit later. 'Thanks!'

She smiles. 'They're the best roses you can buy.'

'I know.'

'You deserve them. You've been a good friend to me.'

'Thanks, babes,' I say.

We hug.

Over her shoulder I see Sooz and Jamie. Jamie is making pretend growling noises at Sooz. Rip-yer-clothes-off growly noises.

Red roses (3)

We're back at mine and I'm putting the roses in a vase.

I'm so touched – I know that Sasha must have spent her entire week's allowance on them.

She and I are talking about Riggs.

'He's so in love with himself,' she says. 'I bet every time he goes past a mirror he blows a kiss.'

'Bet he's Taurus,' I say.

'Really rates himself.'

'Definitely Taurus!'

Sasha looks at me as if trying to weigh me up. 'I was tempted, mind.'

'*Were* you?'

'But only for about three seconds. I mean, have you seen the unbuttoned shirt thing?'

'That's so last century!'

We share a smile.

Maybe we really are best friends again.

Red roses (4)

Sasha asks me to go to a party with her. One of Riggs' music parties.

I deliberate for a while and end up thinking, what the hell.

It'll be a chance to:

- ★ Make up properly with Sasha;
- ★ Cut Riggs dead;
- ★ Maybe get off with some beautiful young DJ.

Once there, I lose Sasha almost immediately. Or she loses me, I'm not sure which.

I get a drink and find myself standing next to Ginette,

Riggs' gay secretary. She's talking to her girlfriend and this is what I hear.

Ginette: 'Up to his tricks again.'

Fem: 'Unbelievable.'

Ginette: 'The younger they are, the better he likes it.'

Fem: 'Straight men are such bastards!'

Ginette: 'Had to send her roses from the account. "Twelve red roses for a talented lady" the note said. Ha!'

Fem: 'He must be sick.'

Red roses (5)

I storm through the club looking for Sasha. When I find her, she and Mr Smoothypants are chatting, looking at each other and practically dribbling.

'Special friend?' I shout at her. 'Yeah, right!'

'What are you talking about?' Sasha asks.

Pulling her away from Riggs I spit out, 'Twelve red roses ring any bells?'

'OK, he did send them – but I wanted you to have them,' she says. 'You deserve them more than I do.'

I laugh. 'Rubbish! You just needed to get rid of them before Rob saw them.'

'No,' she protests. 'I wanted to give them to you. You're my best friend.'

I shake my head. 'Why is it I don't believe you?'

'Please, Nicki. Why are we letting that creep get in the way of us?'

'*We*? Excuse me?'

I leave.

If she is a true friend, if there really is nothing going on between her and Riggs, she'll leave him, and the party, and come after me.

She doesn't.

As I reach the corner and look round, I see her standing there. With him.

And they're kissing.

I go to Dad's flat. And spend half the night crying on his shoulder.

Morning

Dad comes in with a mug on a tray.

'Tea. White. One sugar.'

'Coffee. Black. Three sugars.'

'Oh yeah,' he nods.

'You're going senile, Dad!'

'Feeling better?'

I sigh. 'Sorry I was in such a state. I don't usually... you know...'

'That's OK,' he says. 'Stay here whenever you want, OK?'

I am about to ask him what's going on at his office when the phone rings. He makes no attempt to answer it.

Someone leaves a message: 'This is Craig from Notting Hill branch again. We're still waiting for you to return our call regarding the outstanding loan. Please ring me urgently.'

'What's up?' I ask him. 'What's really up?'

'You know,' he says. 'Cash flow problem. Nothing serious.'

Hmmm.

Sasha

She must have been hanging about waiting for me, because as I get close to the café she comes out of nowhere and starts walking along with me.

'Don't you think this is getting ridiculous?'

'Not really,' I say.

'OK. I'm out of order and I'm sorry about the flowers.'

I give her a sideways glance. 'I really thought you'd

bought them for me.'

'I'll buy you some more.'

'Don't be daft!'

'Look, I'm really sorry. Forgive me?' she asks.

I put my head on one side. 'Not sure.'

Sasha nudges me. 'Remember primary school?' She extends her little finger, 'Make up... make up...'

'... never do it again!' I finish.

'Promise!' Sasha says.

We laugh and go in the café together.

It feels good.

Guess I'll get over Riggs. I always do...

Also available from Channel 4 Books

AS IF jamie & sooz: love hurts

Jamie wants Sooz to open up; Sooz wants
Jamie to grow up. But we can't always get
what we want, as Jamie and Sooz discover.
This is their story in their own words.

ISBN 0 7522 6201 7   £4.99
Order your copy direct from the
Channel 4 Shop on 0870 1234 344.
Postage and packing is free in the UK.